ERICA M

A Lobster Tale

First published by Dean Park House 2022

Copyright © 2022 by Erica Manwaring

This novel is entirely a work of fiction. The names, characters and incidents portrayed in it are the work of the author's imagination. Any resemblance to actual persons, living or dead, events or localities is entirely coincidental.

Erica Manwaring asserts the moral right to be identified as the author of this work.

First edition

ISBN: 978-1-7398380-2-7

This book was professionally typeset on Reedsy. Find out more at reedsy.com

For my Scriva writing family
without whom none of this would be possible

Prologue

Hi,

Thank you for opening this letter. Not many people get handwritten letters these days so maybe it was the surprise. Maybe you're wondering if I'm a long-lost cousin writing to inform you that you've inherited a house in Provence. Nope, sorry. But I am writing to give you something. Something that I think is better than a house in Provence.

My name is Laura. You don't know me, we've never met. But you picked up this package and that means you want to hear my story, and that's a start. It's a story about how people change. How I changed. I spent the first part of my life allergic to people. No, not allergic as such, just avoidant. But that all changed and the point of this is to explain why; and how.

For now, just read the book that comes with this letter. It will explain everything. Once you've read it there's a small envelope in the back. In it is something amazing, and disgusting. Don't open it yet.

All will be revealed, and it will change your life, if you want it to. It changed mine.

Love,
Laura

Chapter One

It started with an itch on the back of my neck. A little tickle, a tiny irritation. It had been there, on and off, I think, for the entire day. Sitting on the bus, looking out into the cold grey evening, trying to block out the feel of the other person's leg pressed into mine, it had become a continuous niggle. Mostly because I was too crushed up against my seatmate to reach up and scratch it.

I watched the passing houses to distract myself, brightly lit windows filled with people having dinner with family, with friends. Like a puppet show.

The weekend was looming. It had to be filled. I knew the drill. Go for brunch, go for a walk, decorate something. Take up a hobby, start a blog, spend a little time with TED and his excellent friends. Go to the cinema, watch something explode. Every weekend, more of the same. Just as it should be.

According to some study I read, human happiness levels are a bit like a thermostat. No matter what happens you have a predetermined setting, and you are likely to continue to return to that at every stage of your life. I was probably as happy as I was ever going to be. Those people out their living exciting lives – celebrities, entrepreneurs, millionaires – weren't any happier than the average medieval peasants eating swill out of a bucket. Which made me wonder why anyone bothered.

But, you know, convention.

So, I would get up and get dressed – very important for one's mental health - I would eat a healthy breakfast courtesy of Mr K and a cow and fill my days with slightly useful endeavours. Read books; water my ficus. Volunteer at the local community centre.

It better when I could just be on my own. It was nice having Charlotte as a friend and Callum was fine for a flatmate but like everyone, they liked to talk, and the scripts were endlessly repetitive.

"Hi, Laura, how's it going?"

"Fine thanks, how are you?"

"Good, what are you up to?"

"Not much, you?"

"Not much."

It reminded me of the thing gorillas do in their nests, combing through each other's fur to find the nasties and lift them away. It was expected and I always followed along, but I never got the benefits – I was just not that kind of ape.

We pulled up to another stop and the person next to me finally moved. Which was lucky because the tickle had become the scratching of the devil's fingernails. I reached back, ready to claw it out of me if need be, and found a lump.

I went cold.

I explored it for a moment, circling the peak, then pressed down to gauge the solidity. It was pretty big to be something that had not been there an hour before.

As soon as I got into the flat, I asked Callum to look at it, but all he saw was a spot, red and angry. He suggested washing more often.

In case he was right, I washed myself four times that night using body scrub, micellar water, pore cleansing gel.

Callum was already gone when I came through for breakfast. Lawyers had to be in super early, apparently. Especially the kind who worked for the common good and don't get paid enough not to need to share their flat with a stranger. Which defeated the point of being a lawyer as far as I could see.

My job was decidedly less worthy. I was on my fifth year of my second sales job. I was one of those people who phoned you a month after you had put in your first order and convinced you another case of wine was the only thing missing from your life. Not cold calling, thank god, I had progressed on from that – a reward of sorts, I guess.

Next step up from my job was the kind where you have an appointment. The kind where you sell business things rather than lifestyle ones. My mum was holding out for the day when I was promoted. She would think of it as a sign I was getting my life together. To be fair, the commissions would be better and the conversion rates were higher. I could maybe afford a holiday, maybe Charlotte would go with me, or… yeah, maybe Charlotte. But I was doing fine where I was. No need to rock the boat.

The building where I worked was squat and square. Some architect had clearly liked Lego a little too much as a kid. It had rows and rows of identical windows, plenty of light and a decent view.

If you sat near the middle of the building, far away from

3

all that, it was quieter. People seem to gravitate to light, and each other, I've noticed. If you pitched it right you could find a space with just enough light but no people. I loved spaces like that.

Three calls in and finally someone said they wanted to hear more. I turned to page four of the sales script and started injecting greater warmth into my tone.

"Let me tell you, Steven, about one of my favourites. This wine is unique, not unlike the Pinot you enjoyed so much last time, and Bulgarian, so you won't find it on the supermarket shelves. Lucky for you, we've got a special deal on right now."

My boss, Barry, was over on the next aisle, helping one of the newbies. I gave him the thumbs up and a smile. He nodded and turned back to the teenager in the headset. He was so strange.

The caller asked a few more questions. I used his name often. Luckily, it was right in front of me on the screen. I was horrible at names, but Barry was always talking about how sales were made on relationships. Rapport. Rapport. Rapport.

I didn't buy into the theory.

This guy wasn't going to buy anything. I closed out quickly and pushed the button for the next call. It rang.

Barry came over. He was curious at the best of times. Intrusive, you might say. But he was the one who made the decisions.

"How did that go?" he asked, pointing at the last call record.

"Fine," I said over the next call ringing out. "Not a contender."

"OK, great. Can I get you to come over with me?"

Oh no. But it was his job. He was supposed to Coach and Mentor us – provide expert guidance from his many... months... on the job.

"Sure," I said and walked over to where Barry was looming over the very young-looking girl.

"Laura, this is Cassie."

I smiled at her. She smiled back. Neither was real.

"Laura is one of our longest serving sales associates, Cassie. She's been with us three, no is it four years now?"

"Five years."

Cassie's eyes opened wider. Barry didn't seem to notice. "So, Laura, care to share your secrets with the new starts?"

Oh god. "Well, Barry, making sales is all about numbers. Set yourself a target to make a hundred calls. Of that maybe twenty will answer, three ask for more details and one or two will buy."

Barry was smiling. "Well, yes. But also focus, always, on rapport."

"Or get quicker at the scripts and get your numbers up to 120 and up the sales. Stay late, work faster, get off the phone quicker, you up the sales."

Barry was frowning at me. It was a bad frown. I thought back to his first rousing speech when he had joined the company.

"And of course," I said warmly. "It's important to inject warmth and humanity into what you are saying. It helps people feel comfortable and trust you more. And people who trust you will buy from you. Right, Barry?"

"That's right, Laura. Excellent point well made. Thank you. We won't keep you from your targets."

I sat back down. This is why I didn't like going off script. It got you into trouble, and kept, consistently, preventing a promotion. I had done better with Barry than the last three. He liked me. Hopefully I hadn't just ruined it.

Sod it, I was going for lunch.

My favourite cafe, around the corner from work, was a little hideaway from the world. The decor was tired, and the tables were sometimes grubby, but the food was good and there was never anyone sitting in my seat.

The guy who ran it had never tried to make friends with me or ask me for my Twitter handle. He understood the value of anonymity. I'd been going there every other weekday for five years and he'd never once asked if I wanted the usual.

I was a little in love with him.

I was eating my usual, a sandwich I'd decided on during my first visit here. Sandy thought it was weird to eat the same thing every day – add it to the pile, sister – but I liked not having to think about it. When something is nice it doesn't stop being nice just because you have it every day.

Outside in the busy street people and buses rushed around importantly. Then there was me, quietly reading my newspaper, carefully detached from it all.

When I checked again in the morning the spot was gone. Because it had hatched.

As I caught my eye in the bathroom mirror that Saturday morning, I watched a little insect crawl out of my hair. A tiny body, black and scaly with long feelers at the front and two tiny claws. It looked like nothing so much as a miniature black lobster.

I should have yelled. Maybe danced around like a bullfighter and wrenched the thing from my head.

I didn't. It seemed oddly familiar to me. An inky crustacean born of my own body.

I looked at it. It looked at me. Then it climbed back between the strands of my hair. I could feel little pink pinpricks track across my scalp – then it settled near my left ear. I thought I could hear a breathy sound, like a whisper on the edge of hearing but the harder I tried to listen the quieter it was.

I spat toothpaste foam into the sink and went on with my day.

Callum was making breakfast. He always put everything out on the counter, bowls, cutlery, milk, even if he wasn't using it, like a B&B. He was the type to brew a full cafetière and heat up the milk. For Christmas I was going to get him a set of doilies.

He stared when he saw my mussed-up hair. I dreaded to think what he would say if he saw the lobster. He likes to see people taking care of themselves. He pushed an empty bowl and a packet of cereal towards me. I ignored them and made myself a cup of instant coffee.

"What are your plans for today?" he asked politely. The kind of conversation you'd expect from flatmates who hadn't known each other long. I was grateful, after Dan happened, that his friend of my friend had heard I was looking for somewhere to stay. And that my friend of his friend had heard he was looking for a flatmate. In that sense, we were the perfect match.

"I'm seeing my sister for brunch," I replied, politely.

"Lovely," he said, showing how we barely knew each other. "Have fun."

"Thanks."

He put his empty bowl carefully in the dishwasher, wiped down the counter, put my unused bowl and the breakfast offering back in their rightful places and left the house.

I finished my coffee at the counter, afraid to venture out into the pristine sofa area. After a while, I took my lobster back into my room and we got dressed together. I pulled out my favourite hoodie but, on second thoughts, chose a blouse and jeans. Not a good idea to embarrass my sister.

When I arrived at the fancy Morningside bistro, Sandy was already sitting at her usual table, feet crossed neatly underneath the blonde wood chair. The serving staff were watching her lovingly from the other end of the cafe.

Sandy smiled when she saw me, like a shark. "Morning, Laura."

I do so hate my name. Sandy got Alexandra. An exotic name. A name that can be shortened in about a thousand different ways: Alex, a grown-up professional type; Sandra, sensible shoes, and book clubs; Lexi, a blonde roller-derby troupe leader. She could have been anything. You can't shorten Laura. It's unchangeable. Immovable. Dull.

As I sat down the gorgeous young waiter brought over her egg-white omelette and placed it down next to her cup of herbal tea. She smiled up at him with genuine warmth and he was caught for a moment in her solar rays, helpless.

She handed me the menu. I put it flat on the table and folded my arms on top of it, pulling the sleeves of the top over my hands. Should have worn the hoodie. I asked for coffee. The waiter didn't even look at me, just nodded.

"How are you?" Sandy said. Good opening gambit.

"I'm fine," I said.

"Eat something."

"No, thank you."

She sighed.

Distraction was usually a good ploy at this point. "How's Alan?"

"He's fine. Why aren't you eating?"

"I'm not hungry."

"Why not?"

The usual sharp retort lined up on my tongue, but I felt a little twinge on my scalp. I nearly reached up to scratch but then remembered my lobster.

Sandy didn't wait for me to speak. "Is it the money thing? Because you know I'll buy you breakfast if you need me to. You just have to ask."

The lobster dug in its feet, making my breath catch, preventing me from replying. My hand flew to my head and rubbed at the sore spot.

"Have you spoken to Mum?" she asked next.

"Not yet."

She eyed me scratching my head. "She's worried about you. We all are." *We*.

"I'm fine."

She waved a fork at me and then seemed to regret how it made her look. "You don't look fine."

"Thank you."

The waitress arrived with my coffee. She was stunning and tall. As she put the cup down, a dull-looking bracelet cuff slipped out of her sleeve. It was clamped tightly to her skin and made of spikey, rusty metal. But her top didn't seem to know it was there. It slid over the rough pitted metal like it was silk. The waitress saw me staring and hurried away, pulling her sleeves down over her hands. I could still see the shape of the cuff under the fabric.

Sandy kept talking. She talked about the weather, about a new cafe that had opened near her, how she had seen a famous American actor in town last weekend, that Alan had a new pair of shoes that were giving him blisters. There were pauses for me to speak, spaces for me to say something. An easy script, simple to follow. A conversation meaning nothing. Passing the time.

Sandy took a drink of her tea. "Dad's been emailing again." So the pleasant part of the meal was over.

"Yes, I know."

"He's says he's coming to visit."

I nodded.

"You didn't reply, did you?"

"No," I said and then couldn't help myself. "I will though."

"Why?" It was a harsh, gunshot response. Shrapnell everywhere.

I didn't reply.

She sighed and put her knife and fork neatly down on her plate, next to the half-eaten omelette. "Well, if this is the mood you're in then I'll get going. I have a lot of things to get done today."

She unfolded a twenty-pound note and wedged it under her plate. She pointed at my phone, lying next to my arm. "Call Mum," she said. "Don't be so cowardly custardy."

My mouth twitched up at the old childhood insult. I felt bad, then. It wasn't her fault I was like this.

As she stood up, I noticed she was wearing a strange dress. It was a navy wrap dress, so far so normal, except that stitched into the front was the silhouette of a much slimmer woman, picked out in highly visible, shiny, gold thread. Weird.

"Sandy?"

She turned back in the middle of putting on her long swingy coat and raised her eyebrows to say, go on.

"How long have you had that dress?"

"This dress? Forever. You've seen it before."

"I have?"

"I wore it to your birthday. Thanks for remembering." She sounded irritated. I hadn't meant to be irritating.

"It's nice," I said, to placate her. Something about the stitching jostled my tongue. "Very slimming." She paused and gave me a look, but I was as surprised as she was. Why had I said that? Then she smiled.

"Thank you," she said. As the coat folded across her and she swished out of the cafe I saw the gold threads were a little less shiny than before.

I felt a twitch in my hair and tried not to scratch it. What was going on?

I went into the bathroom and turned my head upside down over the sink, ruffling my hair, trying to work it loose. But nothing fell out. Unless this was all in my head. Nothing to see here. At least I had left things OK with Sandy. Damned if I was going to phone Mum, though. I'd go to the cinema, eat popcorn, watch something explode.

Chapter Two

The film was reassuringly explosive. The bad people died, the good people won. All was right with the world. Until, as I made my way home from the cinema, I found myself on a video call with Mum. I had turned my phone on when I emerged and it had a message. *Call Mum or I'll conference call you both. Sandy.*

"Bumpie, darling," she said, her face looming huge on the screen. "Finally."

Really, Bumpie? Still? "Hi, Mum. How are you?" I smiled at her, trying to imitate Sandy's rays of sunshine. She looked alarmed. Maybe too much.

"More importantly, how are you?" she said.

"Fine," I muttered.

"Thank you for calling. I wanted to show you something." She held up something big and plastic. But the plastic thing was not what caught my eye.

There was a something, someone, sitting on Mum's shoulder. It was fading in and out of visibility. It was hunched and wizened; it looked like a little gnome from a fairy tale, and not the modern, happy sort. It was crouched close to her neck and whispering into her ear.

"Are you alright, Bumpie? Why are you squinting like that?"

Did she not feel it sitting there, or hear it? Unless she already knew about it. Unless it was there by choice. What the hell was going on?

"Mum, can I come and see you?"

Mum's eyebrows went up and the little gnome turned to look at me. Its gaze was sharp. I tried to ignore it.

"Of course," said Mum. "When?"

"Now?"

"Lovely! I'll expect you very shortly." I let the phrasing pass me by. This seemed, bizarrely, to please the gnome. As Mum stabbed ineffectually at the end button, I stared the little gnome down.

First Sandy, now my mum. It was too much of a coincidence that the little lobster-thing had turned up just before this.

My mother's house was, as always, neat as a pin, the multi-coloured carpet freshly hoovered. The front door had a little brass plaque saying, "The Robinson's, 23". I kept telling her it was identity theft waiting to happen, but she said I was being paranoid. Maybe if I got Sandy to tell her she might take it down. Or at least correct the apostrophe.

She ushered me in and handed me the piece of plastic that she'd had in the call as if it were the Turin shroud. It was a spiraliser. I made some appropriate noises which seemed to be all she was looking for and allowed us to move on to the making of the tea.

While she bustled with the kettle, I watched her from the kitchen table. The gnome was still there in person, sitting on her shoulder. It was gnarled and hunched and had one hand gripping her ear and was talking into it.

Something tickled on my scalp. The lobster was still with me. I ran my fingers gently through my hair and came out with it gripping my little finger. It waved its feelers at me.

Time to test the assumption that this was the lobster's doing. I plucked it gently from my finger and placed it on the cork mat in the middle of the table. It turned towards Mum, clicking its little claws.

The gnome had disappeared. There was only my mother pouring boiling water into the teapot, her back ramrod straight.

All I had to do to stop this nonsense was to leave it there, on the table, and just walk away. The little black creature took a step towards me then raised its front feet expectantly. Its feelers waved in a friendly way.

I put my hand down and it hopped back on.

My mother put the lid of the pot on with a clink. The gnome was back. OK, then. The lobster and I gave each other a little nod.

My mother was now selecting teacups. I stood silently and walked up behind her. As I got closer the gnome's whisper became audible: "I cannot believe you are serving granulated sugar instead of lumps. It's a good thing she's family." The voice was old and warbly. It brought back memories of chintz curtains, a rose covered sofa, and piles of *Country Life* magazines. Grandma.

But Grandma was so lovely. She brought fudge. Her hugs smelled like rosewater and wool. Nothing like this little wizened creature on my mother's shoulder. Yet the voice was unmistakable.

Mum turned her head, obviously sensing me standing there.

14

"You alright?"

"Yes, fine."

I reached past her for a carefully folded napkin and brandished it at her. Her gnome fixed me with a baleful glare. I resisted the urge to reach up and flick it off her shoulder and retreated to the table.

Mum followed me with the pot. She gave me a look and then went back to get teacups. We sipped our tea silently. As always there was an elegantly arranged display of biscuits on the fancy plate in the middle of the table. I ate one for something to do.

"So," Mum said, indicating the spiraliser. "What do you think of that, then?"

I examined it and said just the right things. It would be a boon in the kitchen, indeed, and Aunt Cathy would be very impressed the next time she came for supper.

Throughout the conversation the gnome just watched me. The lobster and I watched it back.

"How's work?" said Mum, after we were done with the kitchen implements.

"It's good. I hit half my target for the month already."

"That's good."

"Thanks."

She genuinely seemed pleased. I took the moment of rare praise.

The gnome was staring at Mum, its expression unreadable. It leaned in and whispered something. Mum opened her mouth. "No progress on a promotion, then?"

The gnome was watching me. I sipped the tea. It had brewed and the sharp tannin twisted my tongue. I could feel the usual words in my throat, sharp and sticky. The start of the argument.

But the lobster was watching me too, expectantly.

It was the gnome I stared at as I said, "No," as calmly as I could. "I'm actually happy where I am. But thank you for asking."

Mum and the gnome looked surprised, but the lobster shuffled in a happy circle on my hand. Fascinating.

The gnome leaned in again, I heard the sibilance of its whisper. "Sandy says your new living arrangement is going well," Mum said.

"Yes. It's a nice flat," I said, cautiously.

"It was nice of him to take you in after what happened with Dan."

"He didn't take me in. I'm paying rent."

"It's such a shame what happened."

Here we go. I took another biscuit to bolster myself and the gnome tutted loudly. I took another one.

"What did happen with you and Dan? Did you ever ask him?"

"We grew apart," I said with my mouth full.

"Did you scare him off?"

I snorted at that. "Probably."

"It's just that now you don't have Dan, I worry about you. He was such a nice boy. So accommodating."

"I'm fine, Mum."

She sighed heavily. I didn't realise I was squeezing my cup hard until the lobster scuttled down my arm. Its feelers caressed the clenched fist until I managed to relax it a bit.

But still, I couldn't help myself. "Sandy said you'd been trying to get hold of me about Dad."

Her mouth twisted. The gnome clenched its fists. She looked down at her hands unhappily. "I just want you to be prepared, in case he doesn't make the trip again."

I felt of wave of guilt, then. I shouldn't bate her. It wasn't fair. "It's fine, Mum," I said into my cup. "I'm a big girl. It would be nice to see him one day but its not the end of the world."

"You're right. It's no loss. It's not like he's ever been a proper father to you anyway."

And that was the point to make my excuses and leave.

But when I looked up the gnome had been transformed into a marble statue, all polished glowing whiteness. A woman in robes holding a crying child. It seemed brighter than the room but patches of the marble were scuffed and worn. The child's face was pressed into the mother's chest – the woman had Mum's face.

I was tongue-tied in front its gentle glow. All the tension and heat drained away.

Mum took a sip of tea and broke the spell. "Anyway. You're an adult. You decide what you want, and I'll support you, you know that."

I heard myself say, "Thank you."

Then the statue was gone, and the gnome slowly reappeared on her shoulder. It leaned over to whisper, and she started telling me about her friend Diane who had discovered her cleaner was helping herself to the alcohol cupboard. I let her words wash over me. The attention was off me; the worst was past.

It wasn't until I was halfway to the Tube that I realised that was the first time in living memory we had talked about my father and I hadn't immediately left as a result. In fact, it had been kind of OK. My mother had seemed almost reasonable. Was the lobster affecting her too?

I felt the lobster's pin-prick claws holding tight to my hair. Clearly it wasn't here to ruin me. It was more of the radioactive spider ilk than the parasitic ear worm. It had already helped me get through two entire conversations with my family. Superpower gift.

I experimented on my walk home. As I walked up to people in the street, like a little lightbulb, an image would appear. This woman had a teddy bear cuddling her. It appeared as I got into her personal space and faded out once she had walked by. This guy had a bat following him home, for some reason.

The lobster's influence was local. I could see the visions when I was within about three feet of people. If I picked a target she ran up and down my arm in her excitement. She was such a tiny little thing – I decided, on balance, she was probably a she – the size of a woodlouse and twice as tickly. It should have been disgusting. But she was so cute with her little clicky claws and the way her tail flipped when she was happy.

I sat in an open-air cafe in the middle of the park and watched the people go by.

It was like a circus, or perhaps like living inside a child's imagination. There was a dragon, a herd of horses, a talking cat. One man, striding past my chair, seemingly just in a hurry, was trailing boiling steam. Another walked under a waterfall of flowers. Nice to be that guy.

A couple walked past me; their hands entwined. What no one else saw was the network on silver filigree meshing them two of them together. A thousand threads, gossamer thin, twinkling in the sunlight. One of them said something to the other and he smiled and whispered something back. Another thread appeared above them and floated down to join the rest.

It was magical. Impossible. So many people had so much

going on inside them this whole time, and I never knew.

Back at the flat, I waited for Callum to come home. If my sister had an image problem, and my Mum was at the beck and call of Grandma, then maybe Lobster could help me understand what made Callum have such a stick up his arse.

I pulled a couple of things out of the clean dishwasher and scattered them over the kitchen surfaces then fetched my book and settled down at the counter. I wasn't reading, just thinking back over my unusual day.

Callum came in at nine, fresh from wherever it is he goes after work. As he came through the door, I adopted a nonchalant slump and stared at the book. The lobster made a noise that sounded like a tiny tut, but I ignored it.

Callum came into the living space, his coat already absent. Probably hung on a hook. Probably on a hanger.

"Hi," he said.

"Oh, hi," I replied, looking up from my book as casually as I could manage.

He was already bustling around the kitchen putting things away. His back was relaxed. I waited for something to come clear – some shadowy figure.

Nothing.

I leaned further forward. Surely some ghostly bleach bottle, or looming Florence Nightingale, would be following him around. But no. He didn't even seem annoyed. He calmly put things back where they belonged and gave a tiny little nod.

He started to turn back so I buried my head in my book again. Was there something wrong with him?

"Good day?" he asked. His expression was clear. He didn't sound sarcastic.

"Fine," I said, then winced as the lobster's claws pinched suddenly.

Callum smiled a bit. "Yeah, looks like you had a ball."

I grimaced back. He didn't want to hear about my day. I knew the polite way was to move onto to other topics. "How was…?" But I had no idea how to finish the sentence. Where did he go? What did he do with his evenings? What did anyone do with their evenings? I'm not sure I'd ever asked.

"The museum? Great."

Museum? Really?

"Oh good." Job done. Pleasantries exchanged. I could go back to my room now.

But Callum wasn't done. "They had an exhibition on Japanese Contemporary Design."

Perhaps I'd sounded too interested. He took a breath to continue. Oh hell, he was going to tell me about it. He had already started. Something about blown glass and calligraphy. I tried looking pointedly back at my book, but he had his back turned while making tea. Why did everyone talk to me with their back turned, making tea?

I hoped my lack of reaction would make the point, none of the grunts and whistles that other people use to keep the conversation going.

No, he was content just talking. Selfish. I started to make a move to leave but a sudden pain in my scalp sent me back to my seat. I sat it out, letting the words wash over me.

Eventually he seemed to be winding down. By now he was leaning on the counter holding his teacup. Still talking. He hadn't even offered me tea. Rude.

It seemed like he was nearly done. Then he said, "It's the last couple of days, so you'll probably miss it, which's a shame."

You see, Lobster, being polite leads to unintentional perceptions of interest.

"The next one is on parasites," he went on.

Oh really? "Interesting. What kinds?"

"All sorts, disease carriers, symbiosis, the whole shebang, I think."

"Now that is something I would like to see," I said, wincing at the sudden skittering on my scalp. I slapped my hand to my head. "Does it say how to get rid of them?"

He looked alarmed. "I don't think so. Um, I think that's what doctors are for."

"Doctors, interesting."

Callum had stood up from where he was leaning and backed away to the other counter.

"Anyway," I trilled. "Glad you had a nice day. I'm off to have a bath. Bye."

The lobster didn't appreciate my humour. It scuttled under my pillow and didn't come out for the rest of the evening, leaving me to my fifth reading of *Villette*. Who knew crustaceans could be so sulky?

When I finally put my book down it was still ignoring me, but it came with me when I went into the bathroom. It watched me from the sink where I had put it as I started running a bath. I sat on the loo and studied it.

"Who are you? Why are you here?"

The lobster waved its feelers at me crossly.

"Why me?"

I was talking to a lobster. I mean, what was I expecting – for it to answer back? The running water of the bath drowned out my conversation to the rest of the flat so at least I was the only one who knew I was going mad.

As I undressed it ran to the edge of the sink and stared into the running water. Its feelers stroked the air as if gathering the water droplets. Was it thirsty?

The steam filled the room – I like my baths hot – and the lobster was inching closer and closer.

"No, you don't," I said and picked it up in case it launched itself in. "That would be the end of you."

I ran some cold water into the sink, enough to form a puddle in the bottom and placed it back on the edge, facing in. Its choice.

I shut my bath off and waited to see what it would do. It gave a little squeak and skittered down the slope of the sink, into the water. It came up to its knees and it splashed about in it. I guessed we were friends again.

Chapter Three

Charlotte was another thing altogether. She was my oldest and, to be frank, my only friend. I invited her over on Friday night. I was looking forward to seeing her with the lobster there as my translator.

She arrived with nothing around her at all. No spectres or mirages. I had to check the lobster was still awake. We said our hellos and I got her a cup of tea and some biscuits while she put her coat and two handbags down by one of the chairs. She grinned as normal as she settled on the chair, across the coffee table from me.

We used to party together at uni, back when a skilful repertoire of small talk was all you needed to get invited to all the good parties. Even though all those devoted acquaintances had dropped off over time she still saw me as a source of advice. Every time I saw her there was something else. I would listen patiently to all the tiny, insignificant things that she always seemed to be in a panic about and then I told her what to do to fix it. She was rarely happier by the end of it, but she still insisted on putting us through it, because that's Charlotte.

When I sat down I must have been looking at her funny

because she started fidgeting.

"It's so lovely to see you," I tried. "How are you?"

"Well," she said, picking up her tea. "That's a good question."

She leaned back and took a breath to begin. As she did so, something unfolded in front of her on the table, blocking her. Was it a picture frame? An easel? It was tall enough that I couldn't see her face anymore.

She carried on talking like everything was completely fine. She was telling me about a problem at work with a colleague who was constantly getting at her. It felt weird sitting there opposite a blank, wooden frame while she talked away.

I subtly leaned sideways to see around it. She was chatting on, not looking in my direction. Unfortunately, she looked up then and her face formed itself into a puzzled frown.

"You OK?"

"Yes. Sore leg. Go on."

She started back up again. I needed to get a better look at this so swallowed the rest of my tea, burning hot in my throat, and made an "another?" gesture. She shook her head, barely breaking stride, so I stood up and made a show of walking to the kitchen. She didn't even turn around as I passed her.

The frame was a mirror. She was talking to herself in the mirror.

Was that all I was to her, a body to be present while she talked to herself? I nearly left the room right there and then. But we'd known each other forever and there was such a thing as loyalty.

The tea didn't take long to make. She continued talking even through the roar of the kettle when I wouldn't have been able to hear her anyway. I sat back down with a slump. All this time giving her advice, helping her solve her problems. I may as well have just played a game on my phone and waited for her to stop. I threw in a few *uhuhs* and *mmms* to keep her happy. That seemed to be the sum total that was required of me. Weirdly the lobster was getting agitated. She was dancing up and down on my hand.

Eventually Charlotte wound it up. The mirror scaffolding folded down onto the table, giving me the first look at Charlotte for almost an hour. There were tears in her eyes. Had I completely screwed it up? I should have given her advice after all. Now she was upset. She was going to be even more angry with me than usual.

But instead of being huffy she started laughing and wiped her eyes. "Gosh, that was a long time coming," she said. What was? I hadn't been listening.

"Enough about me, how are you doing? Have you heard from Dan? Did he reply to your email?"

The mirror scaffolding twitched and started to rebuild itself facing me. I leapt out of my seat.

"I don't feel like talking about it right now," I said, hurriedly. "If that's OK."

Charlotte got out of her seat as well. "Of course, it is," she said, hugging me. "I'm sorry for bringing it up."

"No, it's fine. Honestly." I checked the table. The scaffolding was gone, thank god.

Charlotte started gathering up her coat and bags. "I'll leave you to your peace and quiet," she said. At the door she turned around and hugged me again. "Thank you so much for being there for me today. I really needed it."

The *thank you* felt nice. This was so much better than the usual slightly tense goodbyes. This was good.

I caught my reflection in the glass of the door as it closed behind her. I was grinning. I spun on my heels and saw Lobster was dancing a little jig on the coffee table. It was official. She was my superpower.

Chapter Four

People were fascinating. They had been so impenetrable before, like shadow puppets. But everybody had something, good or bad, haunting them. Everyone except weirdo Callum, of course.

Andy, who always sat near me at work, it turns out, was obsessed with Amateur Dramatics. He had a miniature stage and a full cast running lines all day. It was distracting, and not in a good way. I tried sitting further away but he always seemed to be stationed close by.

The cafe was a blessed relief. Cafe Man's companion spectre was quiet and unobtrusive. It was almost impossible to see. The movement was what revealed it. Around his head, like a cloud of bees, was a swarm of tiny objects rushing in circles. No, not bees – an electron cloud orbiting his head.

It was beautiful. Silent and ethereal it spun and flowed. I could have watched it for hours. Every now and again one barely perceptible dot detached from the cloud and darted towards his head, connecting at the temple. His head would still, and his eyebrows twitch upwards. Then he would put his book down and reach under the counter. A notebook and a pen would emerge and he would scribble something down. He would write for ages then stow them away again and go back to his book. Restful.

Other than Cafe Man and me the only occupant was a woman near the door tapping on her phone. She was one of those rare people without an accompaniment, although her alarming asymmetric hairdo was probably enough for anyone to be getting on with. She was sitting quietly, staring into the tiny screen, not a care in the world.

The door went. I was only halfway through my sandwich and the new arrivals brought some of the outside rush in with them, along with a lot of noise. It was two young girls. Maybe late teens or early twenties.

One of them was laughing. The other was smiling; she looked like she was having fun. I could see she was standing in her very own rainstorm, the gushing rain cascading down her head and shaking her to the skin. Little crackles of lightning broke the swirling dark mass into layers. The rain was thunderous and relentless.

The first girl, smaller, neater, prettier, took in the cafe and her face formed into something which resembled a sneer.

"Why are we here, Suze?" she asked her friend. I could barely hear her above the splatter of the raindrops.

"This is where he said," said Suze. The rain dripped off her nose. Perhaps this rainstorm was why her hair was so lank.

"I can't eat in here," said the snarky one.

"I'm not asking you to eat, I'm asking you to wait with me."

I took another bite of my sandwich, but they weren't interested in me.

"Fine," the girl huffed and plonked herself down at a table. Suze joined her.

"You can't stay if you don't order something," said Cafe Man, not unkindly.

Suze got back up again, seemingly ignoring her friend's sighs, and ordered a cup of tea and a brownie. Cafe Man turned to get it ready.

The friend noticed me. She raised an eyebrow. I raised one back. Not the right response.

"Can I help you?" she said.

"No, thanks, I'm fine," I said and picked up my newspaper.

"Ciara, leave it," said Suze from the counter.

From the corner of my eye, I watched Ciara. A ruffle of feathers had appeared around her neck. She was an irate chicken. I tried not to smirk at how ridiculous she looked. She was huffing and twitching, and it occurred to me that she had no idea how to settle herself. Interesting.

I'd known plenty of people like Ciara. Popular, bossy types who took offence at everything. It had never occurred to me that their constant, eternal irritability was involuntary. Surely, I had thought – or maybe not even "thought", just assumed – that anyone that angry was using it as a weapon. Ciara's neck was now bright red from the irritation of the tickling feathers. She was stroking her neck, twiddling with her phone, knee jumping under the table. But the feathers were unsettle-able.

Suze arrived back at the table with her tea. She stared into the cup as she poured it. The rain rushed in with the tea and the cup overflowed, forming a fringe of waterfall swirling into the saucer. She took a sip and seemed to notice that the tea had been supplanted and was now cold and tasteless.

They bent their heads together and their words were lost in the roar of the rain. The dampness pervaded the air.

I tried to go back to my newspaper, but Suze and Ciara were

still bickering. As their conversation flowed back and forth I could trace it by the effects. A lightning strike here, a feather rising in indignation there. Why were these people friends?

Ciara leapt up. I felt myself jump and coughed to cover it, but I needn't have bothered. Suze's rainstorm was too loud for me to hear what they were saying. Whatever Ciara was doing wasn't helping. There was a howling wind growing in strength and the rain was whining around the room. My newspaper was getting damp.

Ciara said a final something then turned on her chicken legs and stomped out of the cafe.

Cafe Man didn't even look up from his book as Hurricane Suze reached fever pitch. The wind and rain became a roar. I could barely hear myself think. The newspaper was whipped about in my hands and threatened to tear.

Enough.

I got up from my seat and fought my way towards the other table. The wind made me unsteady. My feet slipped on the damp lino. I had to push my rain-soaked hair back over my head to be able to see. The rain was a curtain so thick I could barely see the way.

Finally, my arctic trek was over, and I arrived next to her table. A gust slammed into me as she looked up.

"Excuse me," I bellowed through the raging storm.

Phone woman and Cafe Man both looked up. Of course, I was the only one who could hear the wind.

"Sorry to bother you," I tried again, quieter.

"It's OK," she said. Her eyes were glazed and unfocused. She was right out at sea.

What to do? How do you calm a mental storm? She was looking at me blankly. I ran my hand through my hair and, thank god, it came out with Lobster sitting on the back of it. She clung to the back of my hand, her tiny feet digging into the skin. Her feelers blew crazily in the gale.

I needed ideas. Come on, Lobster.

She looked up at me and then back at Suze. Suze's expression hadn't changed though even I knew this silence was unnaturally long. Her eyes were still looking at a far-off horizon.

The lobster made her way down my arm and landed on the table. Instantly the storm disappeared. I gasped as the pressure on me lifted and I had to stop myself from stumbling. The silence was loud as if the storm had never existed although there was a remnant of rain on Suze's cheek. Cafe Man was looking at me curiously. I smiled brightly at him and sat down quickly.

"Do I know you?" she asked.

"No. I just want to help," I said, before I could stop myself. I wanted to get up and go but Lobster was still in the storm. She was fighting her way across the table towards Suze, feelers blowing this way and that.

She was starting to lose traction. Her needle feet were slipping and skidding on the slippery table.

I reached across and hooked my finger under her, pushing her across the table to Suze's hand. The only way to get her there was to push my hand up and over Suze's and then I was sitting at a table with a complete stranger holding her hand.

The storm was back with a bang. I gripped tighter onto Suze's hand. Lobster was hanging on to me for dear life. Her back legs jolted and then she was lifted by the wind. Her claws holding onto my finger were the only thing keeping her from being whipped away.

"It's OK," I said to Lobster. "I'll catch you."

"What?" said Suze. Her nostrils were flaring. Thunder boomed around the cafe.

Lobster gripped tighter. "I can see what you are going through," I said to Suze. I had to focus so as not to yell. "How dark it is where you are. It's like a storm. And it's getting worse. I wanted to say that I can see that and I want to help you."

Suze's mouth formed into an O. Another rumble of thunder, but the wind dropped a notch. Lobster's feet touched down with a prickle.

The rain cascaded down Suze's pale face dropping in staccato beats off her chin.

"Thank you," she said. Lobster nodded.

We sat like that for a while. The rain was still falling but the wind was more of a gust than a wall now.

The phone on the table beeped. She let go of my hand to look at it. "He's not coming," she said.

The effect was instant. The winds fell to a whisper and the cloud shifted from a black and purple bruise to a mid grey. She set the phone down and sighed – a profound noise that blew the rain away from her face for a moment. We sat in silence for a bit longer. My sleeve was soaked through where I was holding her hand again.

"Can I call someone for you?" I asked, eventually.

"No, I'm OK."

I looked at the rain cloud. It was lighter but the rain was still falling in sheets, plastering her hair to her head. The storm wasn't going anywhere soon.

"I think you need to tell someone how you are feeling," I said. "I think it's not good to deal with this on your own. Is there someone you can call?"

"I could call Ciara to come back."

Lobster turned to look at me from her perch on my sleeve. I agreed. "Not Ciara. She's got enough of her own to deal with. She isn't really able to help you. Is there anyone else?"

Suze thought for a moment. "I could call my aunt," she said, reluctantly.

I look at Lobster. She nods.

"Good. Call her. I'll wait."

"No, seriously. It's no trouble. Thank you, but I'm fine." A bolt of lightning arched out of the cloud and grounded itself on her cheek, which twitched.

"I'd like to wait while you call her."

Suze sighed but she went outside with her phone. Lobster skittled back up my arm. I could feel her lifting a wet strand near my ear and she disappeared into my hair. Suze's personal weather front was moving up and down the street outside.

Cafe Man was still reading his book, but I could tell that he and phone lady had both been listening in.

The door jangled and Suze was back. "My aunt's coming to get me."

"That's good," I said. Her cloud was lightening. There were patches of white now. Suze looked me in the face for the first time. Her eyes were focused.

"Thank you," she said.

"It's OK. Do you want me to sit with you?"

"No. I think I'm OK."

I went back to my table. Weirdly my sandwich tasted better than it did before. Maybe rainwater was good for it. I opened my soggy newspaper. Lunchtime was almost over. Had it only been forty minutes?

When I finished my sandwich and got up to go Suze was

still sitting there, her raincloud still with her, a slow drizzle settling on her head. She didn't look up. Neither should she have to.

Cafe Man glanced at me as I approached. "You're all paid up," he said.

"Really?"

"Yup, all good." He turned back to his book.

I wanted to tell him he was mistaken. But he wasn't looking at me so there was no way to start the conversation.

I swithered. What to do?

Lobster gave me a clue as usual. There was a rustle in my hair and a slight tug towards the door.

"OK. Thanks. Bye," I said.

Cafe Man nodded without looking up.

"See you tomorrow," he said.

I was less annoyed at the familiarity than I would have expected. As I walked to the door, I could see phone lady was watching me leave.

Chapter Five

Over the next week the visions just got more and more intense, especially in crowded places. Walking between the clowns or featureless cowls or gibbering monkeys was like reading a Where's Wally book with the goal of finding everyone *but* the hero himself. Lots of places were becoming a tad overwhelming. Luckily, I was practiced at how to avoid people.

On Saturday I went to the community centre as normal. Nobody there bothered me while I sorted and organised donations for the charity shop up on the high street and it was good to be busy and useful.

I was almost tempted to leave Lobster behind. I might accidentally fall into conversation beyond small talk. But I had never left Lobster before. What if she got lonely?

"Morning, Carol," I said as usual when I arrived at the office. I tried my new sunshine smile on her and she smiled back, looking puzzled. No, it was definitely going to have to go.

"Morning, love. Got a huge pile for you today."

I took the pen she was brandishing and signed in. She was sitting behind her desk, her dashing purple fleece like a mayday beacon, mountains of papers sprouting Post-it notes like hatchlings. Callum would pass out in here.

As I handed her back the pen, I became aware of a ticking noise, like a fast-running clock. There was nothing obvious hovering around her.

Carol pushed her glasses up on her head, displacing the purple-rinsed fringe to reveal a startling strip of silver at her hairline.

"You OK?" she asked, squinting at me.

"Yeah fine," I said. The ticking was steady and insistent. It must have been coming from her. But there was nothing. Could these mirages be sounds only? I reached up to locate Lobster behind my ear and, once I got her onto my hand, tried to lean her in closer.

"Oh, while you're here," said Carol. "Do you mind helping with something? I know it's not your normal thing."

As she turned her back to get something from the overflowing in-tray on the shelf behind her, I stuck my hand out in front of me and Lobster finally kicked in. In Carol's back was a key, one of the simplistic ones from a child's toy, slowly turning in a slot. It was making that little clicking sound as it went around and around. It made sense, I supposed. She was always here, rain or shine. Reliable as clockwork.

She was turning back so I dropped my hand back to my side. Would not do to be caught looming over her desk like a one-armed zombie.

"There's a new cabinet come in," she said. It took me a second to understand what relevance that had to me. "It's a flat pack job and both Clive and I have given up on it. Is that something you could help with?"

I liked flatpack that could be done by one person. "Of course.

Where is it?"

"In the Day Lounge."

Oh. That meant going out into the main centre.

Carol cocked her head at me. "You've been coming here for four months. It's about time you stopped hiding."

I wasn't hiding. I just wasn't prepared. What if they tried to talk to me and I didn't know what to say? I hadn't had any time to work out the script for this kind of thing. But I couldn't find a good argument against it, not one that she would understand. The clicking of Carol's key was the only sound in the room.

In the end all I could say was "OK," and took the instructions and bag of screws and dowels from her outstretched hand.

"Thanks, love," she said and went back to her paper mountain.

"Well, this is another fine mess you've got me into," I said under my breath to Lobster as we went into the hall. She waved her feelers at me and scuttled up my arm and into my hair. I passed Clive at reception, who have me a smile. I tried not to flinch back as an enormous phoenix hovering above him opened out its shimmering gold wings.

The lounge was sightly over-named. It was a big carpet-tiled room behind reception with windowed doors and a low ceiling. It had been painted last winter and was now a jaunty yellow. I had preferred the soothing beige from before but then I had never had to use this room before.

There were six people in there as I approached the doors. Shocks of silver hair slumped in leatherette armchairs. There was nothing for it but to creak open the door and slip in. Thankfully, nobody looked up.

I spotted the box that Carol had described, near the patio doors. As I started across the room towards it, weaving in and out of the chairs, I waited for someone to ask me why I was there.

Two of the six were asleep. Another was reading a book and didn't look up. Two more were having a quiet conversation, their words lost in the drapes and the quilted pictures and embroideries hung all over the walls. The last one was watching me from the depths of a huge, red, leatherette chair. When I caught her eye, she nodded and then turned back to looking out of the window. They were all too far away for me to see anything about them.

The box was already open, so I quickly pulled the pieces out and compared them with what was listed. OK, this shouldn't be too bad.

Except that the tool that came in the box was clearly total rubbish. The Allen key slipped and shimmied its way out of the screwhead. It was small and cheaply made.

As I was painfully winding the third screw into place my throat developed a bit of a tickle. I tried to swallow to clear it, but it itched and prickled. I tried a couple of quiet coughs and pressed my hand against my throat, but it kept growing.

I was going to need a drink to clear it.

"Need a hand?" The voice made me jump. It was the woman from the red leatherette chair. She was holding out a bottle of water.

"Thank you," I said and cracked open the seal. The drink slid past the itch without touching it which was weird. Unless it wasn't coming from my throat.

The woman eased herself into the chair next to me. She was going to talk to me throughout this whole thing, wasn't she? The only experience I'd had with this situation was movies and TV. It could be one of two scenarios. Possibly a frail old dear who needed gentle care and attention but had great wisdom. In which case I should listen respectfully at her knee. Or she was a sprightly rebel who was running the place and driving well-meaning Carol to distraction. In which case I should swear loudly and smuggle her out to the pub. What was my role – devoted acolyte or respectful equal?

I needed more information. I thanked her again for the water to buy myself some time and turned back to the cabinet.

"What's that? Hemnes?" she said.

I looked at the sheet. "I don't think so. The instructions are in Chinese."

"Ah, shame. I like a Hemnes."

She was leaning back in the chair. Her expression was bright, her gaze direct.

I guessed at Respectful Equal. "Are you an experienced Ikea builder then?"

"Twenty years of the stuff. They always give you too many dowels. I have a drawerful of them."

My throat tickled and itched. I coughed again and drank from the water.

"I'm Laura," I said to distract myself, and held out my hand.

"Lillian," she said and shook it. Her voice was whispery and hoarse, and her hand was papery in mine. "Can I get you anything else?" she said. "A throat sweet, perhaps?"

She tapped her neck, and I noticed a scar there, pink against the brown of her skin. My throat scratched again. It wasn't my throat I was feeling.

These mirages were physical now, too. Not good. Was I going to start getting other people's diseases, feel other people's broken legs?

Lillian said, "It helps if you don't cough too much, I find."

39

"Thanks, I'll try that," I said. It must be worse for her – at least I could walk away a few steps and the cough would be gone. I wondered what had happened to her. Maybe I could ask. Was that allowed?

She watched as I struggled with next screw.

"Hang on," Lillian said. "I've got a better one in my room."

She hauled herself out of the chair, an alarming operation which took a couple of tries. I wasn't sure if it was the done thing to help so just tried not to stare.

"Carry on," she said. "I won't be long."

As she shuffled away across the grey carpet the tickle in my throat mercifully died. I went back to the screw, but the edges of the Allen key slot were all buckled, and I was worried about destroying it.

Lillian was taking a while. I got up and had a look at a couple of the embroideries so that the others didn't think I was sitting around and being lazy.

As I drifted from embroidery to embroidery lobster started to do her thing. I tried to ignore the spectres as they appeared. The old guy asleep in the corner with his teeth hanging half out was being tucked in by a young woman in an old-fashioned dress. She flickered in and out of colour and black and white, and from a young woman to an older one, back and forth. She saw me looking and waved hello. I smiled back to be polite. She was someone important to him, someone he couldn't stop thinking about. Her clothes flickered between decades but none of them were recent. Hopefully, he was just reminiscing back to a time when he and this woman had been happy. But I knew that was wishful thinking.

I'd been in love before, but I was pretty sure Dan and I didn't carry torches like that for each other. Not even when we were living together.

The old woman reading the book, however, had a completely different vibe. When I passed close enough behind her chair, I caught a whiff of dust and coldness. My skin prickled and I was ambushed by a shudder – someone walking over my grave. In the too-hot room my arms danced with goosebumps. It was a horrible, familiar, empty feeling.

Lillian was on her way back. I could see her through the glass doors. I went back over to our spot and felt a sense of relief as the cold feeling left me.

Lillian had a couple of things in her pocket. The Allen key, which had a long plastic handle – very posh. She also gave me a packet of throat sweets. The cough returned as she handed them across.

"These helped when I had the throat cancer," she said. "Only thing that did. I'd get that cough checked if I were you."

I didn't think that needed a reply, but it was nice that she had said it.

The third thing she handed me was a little model of a sheep made from Ikea dowels glued together and wound around with wool.

"I told you I had a lot of them. This is the only thing I can think of to do with them." She grinned a big toothy grin.

"It's cool. I like it," I said. The basic shape used a fat dowel for the body, spindly ones for the legs and half ones for the neck and head. The end tooling made the perfect snout.

"My son cuts them the right length for the littler bits and my great-granddaughter makes the little pompoms for the tails. We have quite the production line."

"They're brilliant."

She knew I meant it and held a hand up when I tried to give

it back.

"Keep it. What am I going to do with it? My room is drowning in the little buggers."

I grinned at her. "Thank you. And thank you for this," I said flourishing the key. The screw turned out to be salvageable and it was short work after that. Lillian sat with me while I worked.

"Who's that" I asked, after a while, indicating the lonely bookworm.

"Oh, that's Helen. Younger than me by ten years but you wouldn't know it."

I could see what she meant. Helen had a folded in look.

"She's really lonely," I said.

"So are a lot of folk here."

"Are you?" I looked up into her bright eyes. Why had I asked that?

"Sometimes. But I have visitors. And my iPad is a godsend. I play bridge with a distant cousin in Florida twice a week. Don't look so surprised. I had one of the first mobile phones back in the day. Size of a brick. I had to carry it around in a briefcase. Bloody nuisance. These little ones are much better."

I felt a bit stupid then. She was old, not ancient.

"Are you?" Lillian asked and it took me a moment to understand the question.

"Lonely? I'm…" I was going to say, *of course not, I'm young and busy. I have friends and a social life,* but the words wouldn't come out.

"You seem kind of lost," she said. I stared at her head, her shoulders. Did she have a lobster too? Did I have a spectre hovering over me? The thought made me shudder.

"It's alright. Everyone is, sometimes." She must have seen

my horrified expression. "It's nothing to be ashamed of."

"No, it's not that. I'm just wondering how you can tell."

She shrugged. "I've always been able to do it. It's been useful, helped me open a lot of doors. I guess some people are just born with it."

Or are gifted a lobster who does it for them. I went back to winding in screws, but I couldn't relax. What was it that Lillian could see when she looked at me?

Eventually the cabinet was finished, and I stood back.

"Give it a kick," said Lillian. I was appalled.

"Go on," she said. "Just to be on the safe side. You don't want it to collapse onto one of the old dears." That made me laugh and as I laughed the tension fizzled out of me. She wasn't treating me differently or looking at me with pity.

"Fair enough."

I gave it a nudge with my toe.

"Give it some oomph," she said so I kicked it hard. The kick felt good. It seemed solid enough.

"Good job," she said.

"Good tools," I said and waggled the Allen key at her.

She clicked her tongue approvingly.

I pressed the key back into her hand. "Thank you."

So, what now. Back to sorting stuff in the back room again. I dusted myself off but found myself strangely reluctant to go. She was nice. This was nice.

"Cup of tea?" she said. "We've earned it."

"Yeah, why not?"

"It's over there," she said pointing at the hostess trolley with urns, cups and water bottles on it.

As I walked across the room, I couldn't help but look at Helen, still reading her book. I could taste the residue of dust on my tongue as I passed Helen's chair. The wave of coldness was expected, but awful, nonetheless.

"Excuse me?" I said to her.

She looked up. "Yes?"

"Lillian and I were going to have a cup of tea and we were wondering if you would like to join us."

"Who are you?" Helen's face was closed and the cold radiated off her.

"I'm Laura, one of the volunteers."

"I don't know you," she croaked.

"No."

"No, I do not want tea with you." She humphed and shuffled in her chair as if deeply offended by the offer. Clouds of dust billowed up in the air, making me cough. She looked alarmed. "Go away, with your germs." She waved her book at me, sending the dust cloud into eddies and spirals.

"Sorry. Not a problem. I'm going."

Lillian was nodding when I got back with the teas in two identical white bulky mugs.

"Don't take it personally. She's like that with everyone."

"I don't. I just feel bad for her."

She smiled at me but said, "Don't feel bad. That's akin to pity and nobody likes pity. We oldies can sense pity like a dog smells fear. We see too much of it."

She was right. I had dreaded her pity. We drank our tea and Lillian told me about her cousin the bridge-player in her commune in Tallahassee instead.

When the tea was gone, I went back up to the office to drop off the remains of the instructions. I still had a lot of folding and sorting to do. I had gifted Lillian the excess dowels.

After Carol thanked me, I found myself pausing at the door.

"Next week, do you mind if I go into the lounge again?"

She looked up and pushed her glasses up on top of her head. "Of course you can. Been chatting to the residents?"

"I said I would drop in for a cup of tea with Lillian."

Carol smiled, looking insanely pleased. "I'm so glad you enjoyed it."

"Thanks," I said into the suddenly silent office. The ticking sound had stopped. My Lobster must have fallen asleep.

Chapter Six

On Monday I walked to the tram station, little images popping up above people's heads all along the street as I passed. I squeezed through the crowds and ended up on the edge of the platform. I realised that a hazy parade of shadowy figures was beginning to form on the opposite platform.

The distance over which Lobster was working was growing. Had something happened overnight? Lobster had slept on my bedside table, on top of the sheep. She seemed to like the fuzziness of it. Perhaps the wool had enhanced her powers or something. Or I had. Or perhaps she was just growing.

She hadn't seemed bigger when I'd popped her into my shirt breast-pocket this morning. In fact, she had barely moved at all. She hadn't tried to climb into my hair either.

I took a glance as I sat on the tram, but she seemed perfectly normal. A bit quiet. I hoped she wasn't coming down with something.

When I got into work, I snagged my preferred desk and pulled her out of my pocket for a look. She stood completely still on the desk. She seemed exactly the same as she had been. Perhaps a little paler. Perhaps a bit bigger. I wished I had measured her before.

I scratched my hair as I waited for her to wake up or move. I had never seen her this quiet.

Andy came in and sat down three desks away, as usual.

"Morning," I said. "How was rehearsal?"

"Epic. Finally getting my lines right."

I gave him an ironic thumbs up and he laughed.

I got on with the first call of the day. As was now usual I was flying. It was Lobster that was making the difference, I had to admit. I had always been able to hear people's reactions, but I had never thought about what was behind them. I could identify *Impatient* but hadn't thought about what might be causing it. I always assumed they were being mardy.

The scripts I had long since memorised, but now I could switch between them like lightning. It was like learning to dance. This change in tone meant the prospect was bored, but that didn't mean they were a dead end. This one meant they were chatty but had no intention of buying. Now I knew.

Lobster was still sitting inert on my desk. It was only then that I realised I could still see Andy's little internal actor, a little Shakespeare complete with ruff, running his lines. That shouldn't have been happening. Was she able to do her magic in her sleep now? I looked closer. The tiny form was completely still. I reached out a finger to nudge her awake.

Her leg fell off.

My shriek got everyone's attention. I'd broken her.

Andy and his Shakespeare were staring at me. Which meant she was alive. I felt a tickle on my hand. Lobster was standing there. Another lobster? Two lobsters?

There was a long blank moment. Then my brain supplied the answer. Lobsters moult. It's how they grow. I had been carefully carrying around Lobster's discarded shell.

Thank god!

Lobster was doing a happy dance on my hand as I grinned foolishly at her.

She seemed bigger. I got out my ruler and measured her. Two centimetres. How had I not felt her scuttling about in my hair?

Her shell was slightly lighter, slightly more see-through, slightly less brittle looking. I daren't touch it in case I hurt her but the little tinge of blue in all the blackness was very pretty. She glittered in the overhead lights. Fancy.

She wandered across to the discarded shell and poked it with one claw. She reached out for the broken leg and picked it up in her claw. I wondered how she was feeling as she stared at her own broken leg.

She started eating it.

Yuk.

I turned away. Too private, and frankly too disgusting, to watch. I busied myself getting ready to make my calls. By the time I was done, fake lobster was gone, and my lobster crawled up my arm, seemingly as happy as pie.

As my brain settled into the calls, I thought about how I basically knew nothing about lobsters at all.

That night I started, finally, looking for the facts.

"Did you know lobsters shed their shells up to twenty-five times in the first five years of life?" I asked Callum that night. He was watching the news while I was on my tablet next to him. The woman on the TV was talking about climate change.

He seemed glad of the interruption. "I did not."

"And they eat the shell they have just discarded."

"Yuk."

I bristled. "It's not yuk, actually. It's a miracle of evolution."

The side of his mouth lifted as he stared at the TV screen. "Why the sudden interest in lobsters?"

"Oh, um, something I saw on the internet."

"Reddit rabbit hole? They live forever, apparently."

"Do they?" I let my tablet fall into my lap. "Forever?" That was not so good.

"Yeah, I heard it on a podcast. They're basically immortal. If we didn't eat so many of the things, they'd take over the sea because they never die."

"Never?"

"Apparently. You OK?"

"Yeah, fine. I'm, just... forever?"

Was Lobster here to stay then? I'd assumed, what, a couple of years, tops? She hopped onto my hand. She was noticeably heavier, now I came to think of it.

How big did they grow?

The first picture I found was two guys on a boat holding what seemed to be a monster from a sci-fi movie. A lobster almost as big as they were. They were grinning hugely. Lobster was watching the screen. The tag line said it was 40lb. Was I going to carrying a four-foot-long, monster-lobster around for the rest for my life?

I tried not to panic. Maybe her breed was smaller than that. I tried searching for metaphorical lobsters, empathic lobsters, imaginary lobsters, but all that came up were endless debates about whether the sidekick from *The Little Mermaid* was a lobster or a crab. Not helpful.

I slept fitfully that night, dreaming of struggling up a flight of stairs with a giant, clawed monster shellfish strapped to my back, its spiny legs wrapped around me, its giant claws playing like devil castanets, inches from my bleeding ears. I woke up sweating, the deafening staccato ringing in my ears.

Nope.

I had to do something. She greeted me as usual in the morning, but I couldn't look at her. Her tiny squeaks were echoes of the bellows they would become. Maybe if I could train her to walk behind me like a puppy or stay home and be housetrained. How do you train shellfish?

I tried ignoring her all morning, putting her down on the desk as often as I could without offending her. She seemed even clingier than normal, clutching tightly to my jumper.

At lunchtime I skipped the cafe and went to Deep Sea World, perched on the edge of a cliff a short train ride away overlooking the Firth of Forth. It cost a fortune to get into, but proximity was everything.

The rockpool was surrounded by children, excitedly leaning over the barrier to poke and prod. Each of them looking seconds away from falling in. There was a guide nearby and I headed straight for him.

"Hi, do you know anything about lobsters?" I asked.

"A little," he said, pushing his long hair out of his watery eyes. "But Bill is our crustaceans expert. He's doing a talk at three."

"Is he around now?"

The guide's Adam's apple looked annoyed. "I think he's on his lunch."

"Could I speak to him?"

"He's on his lunch."

"Right, sorry." I looked at him closely. There was a school of fish circling his head. I hadn't seen them before because they blended so well with the aquarium decor. They were swimming about excitedly eating something which turned out to be coins, dripping one by one from above. Each time a coin appeared they fought over it, hungrily gulping it down.

I fumbled in my pocket. "Please. My friend rescued a lobster, and she doesn't know what to do with it." That got his attention. "She wants some advice and I work nearby."

"She could give us a call. The number is on the website." His voice was much friendlier.

"But I'm here now." I reached out and put a £20 note in his hand. "Please."

At that he got straight on his walkie-talkie. Bill came down five minutes later. I passed the time staring into the rockpool. There were no lobsters in there, but a crab had a staring match with me.

"Hello?"

Bill was tall and gangly with a bald head. He had a lobster on his shoulder. I gaped at him.

"You have a lobster," I blurted.

"Huh? What do you mean?"

Or maybe not. I eyed it sitting there on his shoulder, big and red. It raised its claws at me. Bill turned his head to see what I was looking at but clearly he couldn't see it. Could he be unaware that it was there?

He cleared his throat. "I've got a couple at home if that's what you mean. And I'm doing my PhD on them."

Oh, his lobster was representing his obsession. Shame.

"Sorry, that's what I meant. I need to ask you a couple of questions."

He nodded. What to ask first? Which question would be least likely to make him run from the building crying witchcraft?

"Are lobsters particularly emotional creatures?"

51

"Emotional?" Oops, that had worried him.

I plunged on anyway. "Are they empathetic?"

No, that didn't help either. Bill was looking at me oddly. "They're friendly if that's what you mean. My two are a mating pair and they seem very fond of each other."

That's a no then. Bill started making that little shuffle people do when they're trying to think of a way to excuse themselves. I had to be quick.

"Are they immortal? My flatmate said he had read something."

Lobster turned on my shoulder, I could feel her pinpricking feet. Her feelers were waving towards my face. No hiding my concerns from her.

Bill looked a bit more comfortable with this one. His shoulders unclenched and he began speaking in what I assumed was his tour-guide voice.

"There is a common myth that lobsters live forever. In fact, they don't but their cells and organs don't age like ours do, just repair and renew for as long as the lobster lives."

"How long would you expect a captive lobster to live?"

"Usually about fifty years. Some longer but that's about what you'd expect."

Fifty years! No getting away from it, Lobster was now my pet for life.

"How big will she get?"

"Who?"

"My lobster?"

"Oh, you have a lobster. Why didn't you say?" He fully relaxed then. Why hadn't I said? "What kind?"

I shrugged, trying to look clueless rather than insane. "That's why I'm here."

"OK, come with me."

He led me down a corridor, away from the crowds of kids and into an office. He got a book down from a shelf. "Here, take a look."

A book on lobsters. Big red and black behemoths, with club-like claws and feelers like battering rams. I gulped. He opened the tome on a page of pictures.

"What colour is she?"

"Black. But after moulting she was kind of a bit blue."

"How old?"

"Three weeks."

"OK, does she look like this?"

He turned the book around and there was Lobster.

"Yes."

"Common European Lobster."

Lobster did not like being called common, I noted. She turned away and made her way back into my hair.

"She'll grow to about twenty-five inches if the tank allows but they tend to match their environment. Keep the tank small and she'll stay small."

"OK." Tank, right, of course.

"If you have any problems with her you're welcome to come back and chat some more. But I wouldn't think of her as an emotional pet. They're interesting, fascinating creatures, but she's not a puppy."

"Yes, of course. Thanks."

As I left the aquarium, I checked my watch. Damn, lunchtime was nearly over. I hurried back up the steep slope to the train station.

Chapter Seven

By the end of the week, I was on a roll. Barry was watching my numbers. He loved his numbers. Not so wrong for your elite sales team after all, huh, Barry.

At 3pm on the Friday he came over to my station. I had just received a text from Dad with his flight times so I didn't see him coming over and his voice made me jump.

"Can I have a word?"

He was smiling. That looked like good news.

"Of course, Barry." I put my headset aside and pushed my chair back a bit, taking the opportunity to flex my wrists and shoulders. Barry would usually pull up a chair opposite and fill in the lucky employee on what they were doing wrong, or right.

"Come with me," Barry said instead, and started walking. Interesting.

Andy gave me a thumbs up. I gave him a thumbs up back because that's what you do and followed Barry along the side of the cubicles. He carried on past his office, towards the stairs.

As he pushed open the heavily sprung fire door he turned and ushered me through first. I almost stopped in my tracks, but that was not done so I kept walking. What were we going upstairs for? I had never heard of anyone going upstairs.

"Well, Laura," said Barry as he started up the stairs, behind me. "You've had another great week. What's your secret?"

"I've adopted an emotional support animal who's teaching me to read people," I said. It was the first time I had said it aloud and I realised it was true, that's why she was here.

Barry was laughing. "Clearly, it's working. What did you get, a dog?"

We had reached the next floor. He held open the door. The offices beyond were surprisingly only two rooms wide. It was claustrophobic after the football-field acreages of the call-centre floor.

"A lobster," I said.

"A...?"

The wall on my left cracked open to reveal a door. A young woman walked out. Behind her I could see a long corridor with thick carpets, vases of flowers and framed paintings on the wall. The door swung closed over that nirvana.

Barry had walked over and was signing something at the reception desk. The receptionist was on the phone, a cherubic baby rocking gently next to her.

"He'll be out in a minute," she said and pointed at the leather sofas next to her desk. Barry was already walking over to them, so I followed. He handed me a paper badge in a plastic holder. It had a clip on the top, so I attached it to my lanyard. It made the whole thing heavy around my neck.

Barry was staring at me. I smiled at him brightly, but he was back to the same expression he always wore. However, now it was accompanied by a giant question mark floating above his head. He was puzzled by me. That's what that look had meant, all this time. How strange.

The door to the luxury corridor opened again. The man who came through was glossy, like a magazine. His teeth were too big.

He had his hand out as he came over. "Laura," he said, shaking hard. "Glad you could come up and see us today."

"Yes, fine, thanks," I muttered, unsettled by his confidence.

"Barry," he said and did the bro handshake thing where he clutched Barry's shoulder as he shook. There was a moment when the hand on Barry's shoulder became an armoured glove, the kind a knight would wear, a gauntlet. Barry sagged under the weight of it.

"Tom, good to see you again." Barry's shoulder sprouted chainmail. His handshake became a jousting lance. The two of them thrust and parried, their horses snorting and pawing the dust.

Tom let go of Barry's shoulder, placed his hand over the handshake and stepped backwards. Barry's horse stumbled and went down on one knee, his lance fell from his grip and he was left unarmed, gripping onto the gauntlet of his lordship for balance.

I blinked and the moment was gone. Tom turned to me.

"This way," he said. He was himself again but as we turned to walk I saw his reflection in the window of the reception area. Plumes rippled in the breeze atop his heavily armoured helmet. Two gold fleurs-de-lis flashed in the overhead lights. His eyes glinted out from tiny eye slits. I had to be careful with this one.

He had turned away from the hidden door and ushered them into the only other visible room, the meeting room next to reception. Clearly this was not a meeting which warranted the inner sanctum. Tom sat on one side of the meeting table and indicated towards the chairs on the other side.

Barry hesitated as I sat down. He was eyeing up a chair at the third side of the table – equidistant between Sir Tom and me. Lobster showed me his inner battle raging but eventually he trotted to his allocated seat like a good knight.

I tried not to smile. It was interesting that I hadn't been part of the joust. Was I too junior, too insignificant, too female? How exhausting it must be for them. She could ask Callum, he might know. But encouraging more familiarity there was probably not a good idea.

"Laura," said Tom. Oh, that's right, the mysterious meeting. "You are probably wondering why I asked you here?"

What to say to that? I had no script for this kind of thing except for a couple of movies about corporate espionage. In which case I should slam my hand on the table and declare I could not be bought.

Perhaps not. Lobster?

Better to play it neutral.

"I'm intrigued," I said, with a nothing smile.

He seemed pleased. Good choice, Lobster.

"Your sales have been improving week on week. Barry here tells me you are one of our most successful salespeople but that you have lacked that certain something which marks you out as a superstar."

Barry shifted in his seat next to me. Lobster noted that he hadn't liked being quoted. Perhaps he had expected a degree of confidentiality.

"OK."

"But he tells me you have really grown these last two weeks. He's seen a new maturity in you. Isn't that what you said,

Barry?"

"Yes," Barry muttered. Another piece of his armour fell with a clatter to the floor. He opened his mouth to say something else, but Tom got there first.

"Which is why we've decided to bring you onto my team."

"Your team?" I said as I heard Barry mutter, "We decided?" next to me. I felt suddenly sorry for him. All that pompous strutting, like a rooster, and he wasn't the top cock after all.

"Assisted Sales."

I was impressed. That was a good stride up the hierarchy, skipping Barry's team altogether. No wonder he was annoyed.

"It's a big leap but I'm convinced you're up for the challenge. It's a big pay rise and you'll be joining us up here on five."

I imagined myself being presented with my very own lance and pony. Perhaps a Shetland with those curtains on either side. Maybe a donkey. My grin was about that, but Tom took it as assent, as he would.

"That's a yes, then," he said. It wasn't a question. Why would it be? Anyone would be thrilled by the offer. You'd have to be mad to turn it down.

"Yes, please. And thank you." Tom was pleased at my deferential tone.

"Excellent," he said and clapped his hands together once. His helmet had slipped to a rakish angle on his head – he was feeling jaunty.

"When do I begin?" I asked, mirroring his seating position, leaning forward on the chair, his snappy dictation. May as well practise.

"You've got a week of annual leave on your old contract. We'll see you a week on Monday. Reception at 8.30. My PA will get you settled – all the boring bureaucratic crap. Laura,

I'm excited about this."

"Me too," I said.

Barry looked lost as we headed towards the lifts, his armour dragging along the floor behind him, slowing him to a shuffle. We stood in silence as the lifts whirred about their business.

"Thank you for the recommendation," I said politely. I'd ignore what he said about lacking a certain something. His reports were why I was there at all.

"My pleasure," he said. But he was clearly still feeling defeated. The lift arrived and we stepped on.

As it descended, he said something small under his breath. It sounded like, "Be careful." Then the doors opened, and he dragged his clanking baggage back to his office.

I went back to my desk. The chair was as I left it, pushed back from the computer. The headset was precarious on the edge of the desk, the wires seemingly about to drag it to its fate. Why was it so uncertain?

I sat down with a thump. Well.

I looked at the brown envelope sitting on my keyboard. The receptionist had pressed it into my hand as we left the meeting room. She had been smiling in a genuine way, like she was glad that I was coming upstairs to join her.

Maybe it was going to be nice.

I opened the envelope. There was a job description, a couple of forms, and a handwritten note. It said *just a few things which might help* at the top. There was a list: dress code, a map of the fifth floor with handwritten labels on it – *coffee machine, ladies, kitchen, recycling* – and some phone numbers titled *best to call for...* and a list for everything from IT to paper clips. Underneath the name Rashda and an extension. *Call me if you need anything.*

That was kind.

The clock had already ticked itself around to 5.25. Only five more minutes until I was done with this floor, this job, for good.

Barry came out of his office, making his rounds. He didn't look over. His armour was back on, tied tight and secure, although his plume looked a little limp. As he walked the floor it started to lift. This was his kingdom. Call-makers tensed when they saw him coming. They sat taller, read more diligently, injected more bounce into their voices.

Mum was going to be delighted. This was exactly what she had been hoping for. Progress. Proof of life.

I was going to need a suit. Or three. I looked down at my black jeans and smart-ish jumper. What did they wear up there for the day to day? My standard kit probably wasn't going to cut it. Maybe Sandy could go shopping with me, pick out my clothes.

A throat cleared. It was Barry. The clock over his shoulder said 5.35pm. Behind him the next shift was already streaming through the door in a kerfuffle of coats and rucksacks.

"Thanks for all your hard work here," Barry said, holding out his hand. The armour had faded, perhaps because lobster was laying low, or perhaps because it was the weekend. He looked different. Kinder.

I pulled my headphones off and unplugged them from the computer on my desk. The next operative would bring their own. It wasn't even my desk, just another space for an endless cycle of people. No one would even notice that I had gone. That was the whole point of the place.

I stood and took Barry's hand. There was no jousting, just a slightly-too-long-for-convention handshake.

"I appreciate that, thanks, Barry," I said. He smiled at me and I smiled back, like none of the last five years had happened.

As I signed out of my station, for the last time, I looked back over the airport-lounge-sized space of blue-rimmed cubicles. The next shift was already settling at the desks; the window seats were already full. I set off for the stairs. End of an era.

Chapter Eight

When I left the office, I turned left instead of right and I went to my cafe; a celebration. As I went through the door into the singed-coffee fug I checked out Cafe Man. Would he be surprised to see me in here so late? After the excitement of last week maybe he would ask me about my day.

He was reading a book as usual. My feet made sucking sounds on the lino as I approached the counter. He didn't look up until I arrived.

"What can I get you?"

There was nothing different that I could see in his expression. No sign of recognition.

"A piece of carrot cake, please."

He nodded in a friendly way.

"Any drink with what?"

I looked at him closely, but aside from the buzz of the cloud around his head there was nothing unusual there.

"Americano, please."

"Do you want milk with that?"

I never do. "No, thanks."

"OK, I'll bring it over."

I could have been a total stranger.

I mean what had I been expecting? A round of applause? A hug? Back to normal.

I picked up a newspaper from the rack on the wall and sat down at my usual table. There wasn't much space in the cafe today. An older man and a younger one were sitting at a table in the corner. Taking up the rest of the available space was a sad-looking elephant.

The younger man cleared his throat and the elephant's trunk lifted briefly. It climbed to its feet and shuffled closer to the table, looking from one man to the other. Whatever it was that was said made the elephant sad again. It sat back down with a whump.

I almost stood up to go over there but Cafe Man arrived with my order. He didn't say a word and I muttered thank you, without making eye contact. Just how I liked it.

The door went and a middle-aged dark-haired woman came in with a blast of wind that rustled the Lifestyle Section. She was over to the counter in a flash with a big beaming smile. In fact, everything about her was beaming. She was like a little sun. What made her so happy?

Cafe Man looked up. Then his face also broke into a smile. That was the first time I had ever seen his face do that. "Irene! You're early today."

"Evan, how are you?"

Evan? His name was Evan?

"Oh, you know, living the dream." He was grinning and Irene was beaming back. What was going on? Were they family?

"What can I get you? The usual?"

"Yes, please, you're a doll. How's Sarah?"

Evan rubbed his hands with his tea towel. "She's good,

thanks. Loving school."

"Fabulous. She's a clever girl that one. I knew she'd take to it."

"Glad you did." They laughed together. Irene got her purse out and slid a fiver across the counter. "Thanks, love."

"No worries, I'll bring it over."

"It's to go today, thanks, Evan."

"Oh? Somewhere better to be?" They laughed together again. Cafe Man's face looked weird, all scrunched and wrinkly.

Cafe Man turned to his preparation area and started making the sandwich. Irene was telling him about a friend she was going to meet. He was nodding back as he put the sandwich together with a practiced hand, like he had done this particular one a thousand times before. But I had never seen Irene in my life.

Why did she have a usual? And what was up with Cafe Man? I thought he was like me – quiet, self-contained. I thought he understood. But he was chatting away comfortably like it was part of his nature.

I watched as they filled the cafe space with buzzing words, grins and beams of sunlight.

No, this was unacceptable. This was my quiet retreat from the world. Now in the space of a week it had been invaded by tragedy and now noisy joy. It was impossible to filter out these people with their thunderstorms and rainbows.

I pushed my cake aside, no longer hungry. I picked up my bag and put it on my shoulder. Cafe Man, Evan, looked up and gave me the tiniest nod, face serious.

I mean, I rescued a girl in front of him last week. What exactly did I have to do to get a bit of friendliness?

As I left the cafe, I almost ran straight into someone. I

apologised and pushed past.

"Excuse me," said the woman. It was her from the other day. The one at the other table staring at her phone. I recognised her hunched shoulders and the alarming cut of her hair.

I looked closer but she still had nothing revealing around her. "Yes?"

"I'm Paula. I was in the cafe the other day."

"Yes, I remember." People like to be told you remember them.

"I'm glad I ran into you. I'm a reporter for ITV and I'd like to interview you about what happened."

"Why?"

"Human interest." She shrugged one shoulder like that was an explanation.

"No, thank you."

She looked put out. I knew most people wanted to be on TV. I didn't. Sorry, Paula.

"I'm interested to know how you did it," she said.

"Really? Isn't it something everyone would do? Societal expectations and all that."

Paula coughed. "It was... different. To what I've seen before."

I thought about the howling wind and lashing rain. That was a good summary. But then, she couldn't see all that. What did she mean?

"I'm sorry, but I'm just not interested," I said.

But she wasn't going to be put off. "Listen, take my card. Text me, call me, only if you want to. I think you could do some good with this skill of yours."

She pressed a card into my hand. I pocketed it and nodded encouragingly. I'd throw it away when I got home.

My mum was overjoyed when I called from the bus to tell her about my promotion. Sandy cancelled a girls' lunch to plan a shopping trip the next day. Charlotte couldn't stop talking about how excited I must be. You're right, I thought, I must be.

When Callum got home, I was sitting on the sofa. I had barely seen him all week because he'd been working late nights. I had my shoes off, feet on the coffee table, staring at the ceiling. I was too tired to even move them down to the carpet when he came in.

"Hi," I said.

"Hi," he said back. "Tea?"

"Yes, thanks."

"Hard day?"

"Kind of. I got a promotion."

He turned around from the sink. "That's great!"

"To Assisted Sales."

"What's that?"

"That's the fifth floor. Presentations to company boards. Business suits and expense accounts."

"The big time. Christ, that's huge."

"Yeah."

He brought the tea over. I accepted it and put it on the table to cool.

"How was your day?" I said. That's the done thing, reciprocity.

"Not as epic as yours. How are you feeling about it?"

How was I feeling about it? Next Monday was going to be something new. I didn't like new and there had been so much of it lately. But this was what I had been aiming at for all those years. I'd figured I'd have had more time, eased into it with a spot of time at the appointments level, time in a familiar place.

"Great. Obviously."

"But?"

I looked at him. Lobster was no help with Callum. There was no reading him at the best of times, but I knew the expression. Open, interested.

"It's a lot."

He sipped his tea and nodded. The silence stretched out.

I guessed that was enough. I tensed to stand but there was something holding me down. The tiniest of glinting chains. It had me attached to the sofa. Lobster.

Clearly, Lobster wanted me to say more. I let myself relax back.

"I was expecting the next level first. The next team. I'm good at what I do. I've never done the corporate stuff before. They're going to expect suits, and presentations, and charm offensives. I do hoodies and scripts. What the hell am I going to do?"

"I thought you were good at charm offensives. You always seem to know what to say."

The chain began to loosen. I could leave now. Except that I didn't want to. It was nice, sitting there.

"It's all an act," I said.

He laughed, as I expected, little realising how true it was.

"Are you worried you can't do it?" he asked. "Or worried you don't want to?"

"I don't know." I picked up my tea and we sipped together as I thought that one through. But there didn't seem to be a conclusion to be had.

"Anyway, that's enough about my day. TV?" I asked.

He nodded and picked up the remote, leaving me to my

thoughts.

Chapter Nine

Sandy was so excited about my new job that she had booked a hairdresser for me and taxis to take us shopping for new outfits. She was in her element. Every time she called me her voice was a little warmer. She invited me to lunch, to strategise and to shop.

It was in the same cafe that she had suggested brunch in before.

I arrived early without meaning to. The waiter was different but of the same breed. This one had a little guy on a surfboard riding what I presumed was a gnarly wave on his shoulder. It was restful watching his miniature surf-dude's long, blond hair billow in the wind. The waiter's own hair was scraped back in a topknot.

I found myself smiling at him and he smiled back as he took my order.

"Can I tempt you with a side order? Maybe some polenta chips?"

I considered it. His surfer waved at me, wobbling on his board as a result.

I stifled a chuckle and managed a "That sounds great." The

waiter took the menu back.

"Anything else you need, I'm right over there." We smiled at each other for a bit. He seemed reluctant to leave, like he was going to say something. But then surfer dude blew me a kiss and the waiter finally turned and left. I felt the residual warmth of his sunny seascape on my face and basked in the glow.

A movement at the door caught my eye. It wasn't the surfer's sunshine I was basking in; it was Sandy's. For the first time in as long as I can remember she was beaming at me.

Dad called. I was in one of the endless 'essential' shops with Sandy buying my new corporate wardrobe. I was trying on another of endless identical navy suits, although this one had the shirt sewn into the trousers, like a babygrow.

"Hi," I said, slapping Sandy's hands away, hoping she couldn't hear anything. Sandy raised her eyebrows and mouthed – *who is it?* She didn't seem to care when I waved her away and went off to browse a section of bright orange skirts and jackets. I turned my back.

"Hi, Laura, I'm so sorry that didn't call you before my flight yesterday."

"That's OK," I said, trying to keep any reaction out of my voice.

"I've arrived safely. Do you think we could meet up?"

Sandy was listening in avidly. "OK, sure." Nice and neutral.

"Great. My connection gets into Edinburgh at four so six o'clock? Where's easy? Waverley?"

"OK, sure."

"Great, see you then."

I hung up the phone guiltily

"Who was that?" Sandy asked, appearing behind me like an oracle. She didn't give me time to answer. "What do you think?"

I turned to look in the mirror. I looked tall, professional, capable.

"I don't know. It's not very me." I yanked the waistline straighter. There was only me, Sandy, Lobster, and the sales assistant in there, but still.

"Exactly. Wasn't that the brief?"

I ran my hands over the trousers. They were attractive. The fabric seemed to be weightless but also pushed me into a sleeker shape. Tom would approve of it wholeheartedly. The thought made my feet itchy.

"I don't know."

"Trust me," said Sandy. "It's exactly what you need to blend in. It's like the uniform. If you showed up in your jeans everyone would stare. In this you can pass unnoticed amongst the enemy."

I caught her eye in the mirror. She was smiling but it wasn't a pity smile. She understood. I felt a sudden urge to hug her but instead let her pay for it with her platinum card and take me out for ice cream. Lobster was delighted. Sandy's halo was glowing, but it wasn't the usual harsh glare of limelight, it was a subtler, yellow glow of happiness.

As I trailed down George Street after her, I marvelled at the change. I thought she looked down on me. But she was happier being allowed to help, even more so than showing off about her successes.

On the way back from the centre of town, bloated with ice cream, I texted Charlotte as promised. She was itching to see what we had bought.

When I got to my front door she was already there. She took the glossy tote bag off me and stroked its satiny side. Why was everyone so excited by expensive office-wear?

We went straight into my room. As I was changing, I called Lobster out and, with her help, Charlotte had soon set up her mirror and was downloading into it. I listened with half an ear, glad for the privacy it afforded me as I stripped off my jeans. The thing that struck me, as I stepped back into the babygrow, was that Charlotte was pretty good at solving her own problems. All that time I had wasted trying to tell her what to do.

"Ooh," said Charlotte, peering around the edge of her looking glass. It dissolved as she watched me. I felt exposed so I shuffled behind the bed a little. "Put on the jacket."

I struggled it on. Charlotte made happy noises and expressed the appropriate amount of desire to pinch it off me and take it home. I nodded and smiled and did the appropriate amount of twirling, but I was relieved to take the thing off again and hang it in the wardrobe, back in its plastic suit bag.

"This was fun," said Charlotte when I walked her to the front door. "We should go shopping together one time."

Maybe I should have told her about meeting Dad too. I wasn't sure why I hadn't.

Chapter Ten

When I walked into the concourse of the railway station the noise hit me like a wall. Hundreds of people going about their day were bad enough, but the accompanying spectres were deafening.

Dad was standing under the station clock, which was suspended from the ceiling in the middle of the huge space like a bulbous arrow. To me it looked nothing so much as a wasp's nest.

Come on, Laura, don't be so cowardly custardy.

The nerves in my stomach could surely be heard above the train announcements. As I walked across the cold floor I had a sudden feeling that he was a stranger to me. That we would exchange briefcases and talk about the weather in Vladivostok in February and go our separate ways.

Yet he was so familiar. His face was more tanned, more lined, than it looked on Skype. His hair was whiter, but it only served to emphasise the green of his eyes. The same green as mine.

Had he always been so short?

"Laura, hi!" he said, a little too loudly, a little too Australian. "How are you?"

I was getting close enough for him to let go of his wheely-trolley handle and lean in for a hug. I felt myself pull back and his arm landed awkwardly on my throat. Less a hug than a half-nelson.

We laughed. He gripped his trolley handle again, as if for support.

"Taxis are this way," I said, obviously.

He nodded and we set off.

Lobster was sitting on my shoulder watching as he tilted the trolley and fell into step beside me. There was nothing hovering around my dad yet, nothing revealing. Perhaps his guard was up too.

The taxi rank was quieter than the noisy concourse. As we joined the queue, I felt the butterflies return. What should I start with? How should I connect with him?

"How was your flight?" The easy words flowed out, unbidden. Socially acceptable small talk. Social grooming. My specialty.

"Fine. Long."

"Did you get any sleep?"

"Business class," he said and shrugged like I knew what that meant.

I made a non-committal noise.

The conversation began to flow freely, easily. So many non-threatening questions and so many easy answers. His house, his job, his wife, his kids, all doing well. The weather *was* shocking. But all the while I could feel the thunderclouds rising inside of me.

Lobster shuffled around in a circle. Her little pin-prick toes tapped out the obvious message, like our own morse code.

"Dad?"

"Hmm?" He looked up from examining the river.

"I need to know why, after everything, why you left?"

"Ah," he said, his expression changed. His hand found its way to the trolley handle again and his palm moved restlessly on the moulded plastic. A spectre began to appear. On his drooped shoulders a curved shape as if emerging from mist. A planet. Earth. It was balanced precariously on the back of his neck, bearing down its entire weight.

I shouldn't have said anything. I was ruining his trip and it hadn't even started. There was a roaring in my ears. Stupid. Selfish. Should have kept quiet.

But I had to know.

I could feel the babble rise in my throat. "I'm still really sorry for what happened. I know I'm why you and Mum argued. But I don't understand why you left. Were you punishing me?"

"No! Of course not. It's not your fault that I left. I'm sorry." Dad sighed. "What that horrible woman did to you. I should have protected you. I couldn't bear to see what it did to you. To all of us. I'm so sorry I ran away."

I could hear my breath snorting through my nose like a horse. "But she didn't do anything to me."

His expression made me spin on my heel and walk. I heard tiny plastic wheels rattle on the pavement behind me. He was following me. I didn't want to see that expression ever again. His disappointment. Maybe if I just kept going I could leave my stupid words behind. Maybe it would fade into the distance enough to pretend I had never tried.

Lobster appeared in my eyeline. A flash of blue. I glared at her. What?

She was floating an inch from my face and raised a single claw, the size of a teaspoon and reached towards me. I leaned back but she was inexorable.

Her claw closed on my nose.

"Ow!"

Through watering eyes, I saw her flick her tail, forcing her forward and around, dragging my face with her. To face my dad.

He was slightly out of breath and his hair had got messy. The glossiness of his clothes was dulled with a sprinkle of drizzle. There was a drip on the end of his nose. Better than the lobster on the end of mine.

"You don't still believe that crap do you?" he asked.

As soon as the words came out of his mouth, I felt like I had been slapped. Like someone had shouted them at me. I could hear the echoes of it in the misty parts of my brain where the blank spaces were.

I pressed my hands away into the knobbly concrete barrier to stop myself pressing my forehead there instead. He put a hand on top of mine.

"Your mum filled your head with nonsense."

I jerked my hands away.

"You're the one who moved to the other side of the world!"

A passer-by looked over at us and walked a bit faster. Oh god. I was just like Suzy from the cafe. I was the dramatic one, still. I should just leave. Walk away. Pretend I didn't have a dad. Be like Sandy.

"Why are you here, Dad?" I said. "To try and cause a fight? To mess things up again?"

The watering in my eyes congealed into the corner and I felt a blob of it escape and run down my cheek. Entirely due to the pain in my nose, but Dad took it another way.

"I'm sorry, Laura," he said. "I was a coward. I have been

for years." He ran his hand through his damp hair, leaving channels of scalp in between. The planet bore down on him and his shoulders dropped even further until his camel coat looked like it might slip from his shoulders.

Lobster pinched hard again but I was done. I reached up and swatted her away. She let go and floated free, snapping her claws at me.

"I have to go," I said.

Dad was looking at me through the rain. "OK," he said. "I'm going to check into my hotel. There's a table booked for us at seven. Will you be there?"

"I don't know," I said. "Maybe. I don't know."

He nodded, sadly. I walked away, Lobster was clinging tightly, too tightly to my shoulder, but I was glad because the pain meant I wouldn't cry.

Chapter Eleven

Mum had been telling the family all about my promotion and everyone was so proud.

"It's been a long time coming, Bumpie, but we couldn't be happier for you. It feels like you are turning a corner."

"Right."

"I also ran into Charlotte's mother yesterday. Charlotte has been singing your praises. Says you have a whole new lease of life. That you've come out of yourself."

"I guess so."

"I'm so proud of you, darling." She genuinely seemed to be. "It's funny. We spent thousands on the best therapists that money could buy to try and fix you, and now it just happens spontaneously."

To fix me. Right. But it felt nice, hearing her say she was proud. So I said, "Thank you."

The dark feeling was still swirling around me and maybe that's why I said, "Something else happened too, Mum. I saw Dad today."

She went still. "Why?"

"Because he flew all the way out from Australia to see me."

I didn't need Lobster to read my mother's warning signs. "Are you going to see him again?" she asked.

"No," I reassured her. "Probably not, I just felt I owed it to him to say hi."

"I should hope not. Why in god's name would you even speak to him in the first place?"

I got to my feet to blow off a sudden nervous twitch in my legs. "Oh, I don't know, maybe because he's my dad."

For most people that would be a good explanation. My mother isn't most people. Her face went squinched and angry. "But why now? You didn't before?"

I started pacing the room. Lobster was holding on tight to my shoulder. "Does it matter?"

"Oh, don't get snippy. You know what I mean." My mother's eyes filled with tears. "You're doing so well. You've got that promotion, finally. You're making progress. Why would you want to do this?"

We lapsed into silence.

"He wants to make it right."

That was entirely the wrong thing to say. My mum's face swelled up like a pufferfish, all spikes and redness.

It was always thus. I heard myself say, "I wish, just for once, you would listen to me."

Her mouth was opening and closing, swallowing gulps of indignation which swelled her head further and further.

I hung up. You probably think that's terrible of me. But there was no other option. Believe me.

I was having lunch in the park when the stench hit me. Rotten food and a sharp tang like the sea. I gagged. It climbed inside my nostrils and singed the hairs.

I looked around but the park had gone dark. So dark, in fact, that I almost couldn't see. I was sitting down so I didn't stumble but the darkness continued to invade until it was so huge and all-encompassing that I lost all sense of where I was. I seemed to be floating – I couldn't feel the seat underneath me, the table had gone from under my arms. I resisted the urge to flail about to try to catch my balance. There was no balance, just this emptiness. No right way up.

I swallowed the lurch in my stomach and let myself drift, succumbed to the smell. A voice echoed through the darkness. He was asking for a newspaper. I tried to turn, to see, but how do you gain purchase when there is nothing to hold on to? Like a swimmer out of her depth, I flailed. I was gasping for air but knowing each breath brought only the putrescence. It felt familiar, even though it wasn't mine, like an echo of something I had once known.

Then it was gone. The light flooded back.

I gripped the table gasping, retching. The clean air swept into my lungs chasing out the foulness, each breath a pure joy.

As soon as I could I looked around. Who was it? Who lived that way every day? Surely they would be easy to spot. A person in that much pain would be a gibbering wreck. Easy to find.

The people walking away from the newspaper stand numbered three. All men. All three were identically dressed in suits and shiny shoes. All three had hair waxed into stylish submission, one blond and two brown. Surely it couldn't be one of them.

There was nothing to distinguish between them. Before I could decide which one to try first, they were gone into the crowd.

Lobster was watching me. I turned to her then.

"There's so many unhappy people." I felt the panic rising. "What am I supposed to do?"

Lobster just looked at me calmly. I knew what she was saying, but I couldn't. Exposing myself on TV like that.

Even if it meant helping someone.

I pushed away from the table, and her, in disgust. Walked away from my lunch, from the memory of the smell, from the feeling of the remnants of that darkness following me. It felt like something had come loose inside of me.

Chapter Twelve

I met Paula at a large noisy bistro near Covent Garden. She waved me over as soon as I got through the door. She was easy to spot with her dramatic hair. There were already olives and bread on the table.

"I was starving," she laughed and pushed the olives towards me. I rolled one around my tongue marvelling at her confidence.

"Order something," she said, waving her hand at a passing waitress. "It's on me. Get a mimosa, they're gorgeous. Or a Bloody Mary."

"A tonic water please," I said.

"And a mimosa. If she doesn't drink it, I will."

I should have been annoyed but she was being funny.

Just to be sure I sat back in the chair and scratched the back of my neck, dislodging lobster from her snoozing site. She hung onto my hand as I brought it back to the table. The room filled with noise and shadows. I focused on Paula to filter them out but as usual there was nothing scary hovering around her.

Paula raised her glass. "I'm glad you're here and that you've said yes. I think this is really exciting."

"Yeah, it'll be good."

"So, what made you change your mind?"

"I thought about what you said about helping people." She grinned and I felt hot with embarrassment. Far too earnest. "Oh, and the fact that my mum wouldn't want me to do it."

"Oh?"

"No. It's fine. That's a great reason to do it."

"Am I causing a problem?"

"No, no. It's not you."

"Are you sure?"

Her worries were circling the table like a brewing tornado. We weren't going to be able to eat a nice lunch until I got this out of the way.

Paula clearly wore her emotions close to the surface. She was so present, so immediate. Not like me who could lock things away in little boxes. Her feelings were oozing all over the table. Her boxes must be made of chicken-wire. Maybe a short, simple truth would ease her worries.

"My mum and I have had a difficult relationship ever since my father left. She thought he was trying to take me away from her. She had his visitation reduced to basically nothing. He lives in Australia now." *And is here right now in this city.* No, better to focus on this.

"Oh, I'm sorry."

"She blames me for him leaving." My voice carried on. "I was a strange, emotional child and it caused problems between them. But she's my mother, so instead of being angry at me, she keeps trying to fix me. Make me more how I should be."

"How should you be?"

"More like my sister. Stoical, capable, popular, normal."

"How does your sister feel about that?"

That surprised me. "I don't know. I've never asked her. I assume she agrees."

But Paula's cloud had eased somewhat, the sunshine breaking through. That was enough.

"You can stop interviewing me now."

"Sorry," she grinned. "Force of habit." The waiter arrived then with the drinks. "Let's celebrate," she said. "Order anything you want."

We had three courses each. I avoided the lobster. By the end of it I was tipsy and stuffed to bursting. Paula was noticeably slurring. We clinked glasses for the hundredth time while lobster danced in drowsy circles around the table. I didn't remember ever having a meal like it in my life. Was this what a girls' lunch was?

Thankfully, Paula suggested coffee. The burnt toastiness of it steadied me. I don't remember what we had been laughing about so much during that long lunch, but I remember her asking the next thing.

"Where did you get this incredible talent from? Have you always had it?"

That sobered me up. I had to be careful. "No. I don't think so. People tell me I was a sensitive child, but I don't really remember it." Oops, too much. "But I'm just glad to help, really."

"So it's an innate thing."

"No, I'm still learning it."

"Well, I'm really glad I was in the cafe that day. I think it's so exciting that we can share it with other people. Help them."

"That's how I feel too. I just don't want people to hurt any more."

Paula raised her glass, and we did another toast. Lobster, my superpower, had fallen asleep on the table. Little champagne bubbles were rising above her head and popping gently in the air.

Paula moved fast. My hangover was barely cleared before I found myself standing in a studio-like room with two strangers, Paula, and a cameraman. A new set of bubbles were fizzing in my stomach as Paula introduced us all. I managed a small hello.

The other couple looked equally nervous. There was Divine, small, contained, staring at her hands, and Andre, a man mountain, staring around the room with a challenge in his eyes. They didn't look pleased to be there, but Paula reassured us all that this was just a little chat.

"Laura is going to listen in to your conversation and just give a bit of feedback. See if she can help you figure out the problem."

"Is she a therapist, then?" asked the large man.

"No, more like a psychic."

I winced at that. Was she setting me up for a fall here? Was Mum right and I was just going to make a fool of myself?

But Paula was brisk and confident. She asked a raft of questions and we all sort of fell under her spell. Within moments the couple were arguing.

I looked back and forth between the two. Spitting bile. The thin silver thread that joined the two of their hands was wavering and twitching like it was going to break. Andre had the end of it grasped firmly and as he waved his arms around it tugged and pulled at Divine like a leash. There was a lot of words being said and a lot of effort being made but that string was fraying. Only I could see why.

Both were talking into mirrors.

I stood up and walked around the room a bit to see what I could see. Neither one noticed.

"You never listen to me," snarled Divine, into the mirror. In Divine's mirror there was just herself. Did that mean she was selfish? Too focused on her own needs?

"All I do is listen," wailed Andre. It showed an older woman with the same overbite as him. She tutted and turned away. "I listen to all the crap, all the time. All you do is dump it all over me. What do you need me for, why can't you just deal with it yourself?"

Divine looked down at her lap. Her mirror face stayed staring ahead. The skin began to pucker and blister and pus fell into her lap. No, not self-centred. Self-hating. Andre's words were making it worse.

Paula and the cameraman were watching the two of them like animals in a zoo. Sitting on their comfy chairs on a little platform like performing monkeys. This was going to continue down this road until they were both beyond help.

"Wait, stop," I said. "This isn't working."

Everyone in the room turned and looked at me.

"Andre, look at me." He did as I asked, looking thunderous. "OK, think about your mother." Lobster jiggled in my hair. "Grandmother? OK, your grandmother."

Andre's mouth dropped open.

I plunged on, "What would you say was the worst thing about her?"

"I don't want to talk about *her*."

"Why not?"

"She's dead."

"Please, just trust me."

He didn't look happy but, after a glance at Paula, who nodded, said, "OK."

I didn't say any more – just waited.

He cleared his throat. "She was formidable, my grandma. She raised me, with my mum, when my dad died." As he spoke the grandmother appeared behind his shoulder. She leaned down, her face all pinched and mean, and started snarling into his ear. "She didn't suffer fools gladly," he continued, sinking slightly in his seat, as if able to sense her. "She pushed me every day to be the best I could be."

"What was the worst thing about her?"

Grandma turned to me and glared. I'd seen worse.

Andre seemed reluctant to speak. He cleared his throat again and the words came out small. "She could be a little harsh. She didn't like people to be emotional. Said she was toughening us up. For what I'm not sure."

Divine was leaning forward on her seat. Her mirror has shifted slightly to one side so she could listen.

Andre chuckled but it wasn't a joyful sound. "My dog died when I was nine and when I cried Grandma sent me to my room for being too noisy. Said it was for my own good and I could come back down when I had pulled myself together."

He was slumped right down in his seat now, his grandmother's hands on his shoulders, pushing him down.

I walked towards them both. "Now imagine you are talking to me but I'm actually a mirror. In the mirror you can see your grandma, standing behind you with her hands on your shoulders. What would you say to her?"

The mirror sprung up in front of me obscuring his face.

Andre nodded and focused. "Why were you so harsh with

me?" he said, his voice smaller. "I tried to be the man you wanted me to be. Tried to be strong enough to deal with myself like you said. But I never was."

"Just like your wife," I said, deadpan.

Divine's mouth formed a shocked O. Her hand flew to her chest. Andre's face clouded. He sat forward, loosening Grandma's grip. "No! D is the best, the strongest woman I have ever met. The bravest."

"What makes her strong and brave?"

"She feels things, so strongly. So beautifully. She loves people hard, even when they can't handle it. She feels more deeply than anyone I have ever met, the good and the bad. It hurts her, every day. And she's brave enough to feel it anyway." Grandma was struggling to hold on, leaning forward over the chair, almost unable to keep her feet.

"But you still tell her to behave like Grandma told you to."

His mouth opened to reply but nothing came out. Divine turned to him, eyebrows raised. He opened his mouth to respond but instead slumped his elbows onto his knees in the chair. That final movement pulled him out of the old woman's grip. "Bloody hell, you're right."

Grandma turned to glare at me, but a wind had started up and was picking her hair up from around her face, distracting her. I could feel it buffeting my face, but I was out of the storm's reach. She clutched onto the back of the chair as the wind began to race and howl. Her feet started to slip, and I fought the urge to dart forward and catch her – she had to go. Then her feet were swept up from under her and a tornado whisked her away. She wasn't going to be gone for long, but perhaps long enough.

Divine had sat forward and taken Andre's hand in his. She

was stroking the back of it with her thumb. "I had no idea she made you feel like that," she said.

Andre covered her hand with his. "I don't want to burden you. You already deal with so much."

"It would help me to know. I can take it."

Andre nodded. "If anyone can, you can. I never met anyone so strong."

She beamed. Her mirror was discarded on the floor next to them, but her reflection was glowing golden. "You're feeling really exposed right about now, aren't you?" she said. He laughed and shrugged, embarrassed.

"Laura, I think we're done here," she said and nodded at me. Her head was up and her gaze direct. I nodded back. As they hugged on the sofa, I saw the silver thread was now twisted around them both like a net. Divine was holding both ends.

"OK," said Paula, suddenly, standing up from her chair. "Thank you both for coming." They thanked me and left the room arm in arm.

I sat back down on my chair; my legs suddenly unable to hold me. So that's what running a marathon felt like. Paula and the cameraman were talking in quiet voices, way off in the distance. It was soothing, like the wind in the trees.

"Well," said Paula, coming up and sitting on the chair next to mine. "That was impressive."

"Thank you." I sat up. The cameraman was gone.

"It's like a miracle." Paula was staring at me like I was some kind of saint. I felt weird. Lobster tickled me and I shifted my head, but Paula's eyes didn't follow me. I squinted to see what she was looking at. There was an older woman hovering in front of me. She was smiling at Paula and dressed all in white, one hand raised.

I cleared my throat and Paula blinked. The woman disappeared.

"Sorry," she said. "It's just you remind me so much of... Anyway. I think this is excellent. Really good. We're going to edit it up and pitch it to my boss. With any luck it'll go into a segment this week."

"On TV? This week?"

"Yup. That's OK, isn't it? Show the world what a bit of empathy can do."

I felt myself nod. We were helping.

The show went out on a Tuesday morning. Callum took the morning off work and Sandy brought over pastries. We had a little viewing party.

As the breakfast presenters grinned their way through the morning show I tried not to look too closely. If this went well, I might run into them on set in the future and I didn't want to know their secrets. Not yet.

The TV was muttering in the corner when Sandy arrived. I was too nervous to get up, so Callum answered the door. She introduced herself to him and they made small talk in the kitchen. I watched them from the sofa. Sandy was even more button-up than usual. Her shiny golden hair, the exact same colour as the spectral stitching on her black trousers and polo neck. Next to her Callum was loose and relaxed, asking her questions in what I called his lawyer voice. They were both smiling but could have been rehearsing a play. Why did people do this to themselves?

My phone buzzed. Charlotte hadn't been able to get time off but was watching secretly on her laptop and live tweeting. She'd written *Only moments left until the debut of Laura Robinson*

#bestfriend #goodpeople.

A part of me was wishing she wouldn't. What if this was awful? What if I came across like a prize idiot? What if they laughed at me? Wouldn't that be better to do in the shadows? But it was daytime TV – surely the only people watching were students and old people. It was a drop in the ocean, barely noticeable in the big scheme of things.

Another part of me wanted to *Like* it but I wasn't sure if that would seem big-headed.

My stomach bubbled and fluttered. Sandy brought the pastries over and put them on the table, just missing Lobster who was waving her feelers at the TV. Between Sandy and Callum they had arranged the pastries neatly on a nice plate. I guess they at least had that in common.

I picked up a pastry to be polite and turned it in my hands, the lump in my throat preventing me from eating it. The interview on the TV was wrapping up.

"It's nearly me," I said, swatting down the nerves.

"OK, coming," said Callum. He appeared out from behind the kitchen counter with a bottle and three champagne flutes.

"What?" he said. "It's a celebration."

I barely heard the pop over the presenter saying my name then the screen switched to the reporter.

Callum put a glass of bubbly in my hand. I tried a sip, but the bubbles stuck in my throat and made me cough.

Through watery eyes I watched myself on the screen. Oh god, I sounded weird. What the hell was I thinking. People were going to see me; they were going to think I was insane. What right did I have to reveal their secrets on national TV?

Lobster on the table in front of me had gone still, her eyes fixed on the screen.

The me on the screen was talking to Andre. His grandmother was still hovering behind him but this time I didn't look at her. His face was thunderous. I read his expressions, the same way I used to. He was angry. Then it changed to confusion, then sadness, then to joy.

A journey that Lobster had made happen.

My phone buzzed again. When I looked down, I saw I had finished my glass of bubbly. I didn't have time to read the message, the TV had switched to an interview with Andre and Divine. I sat forward. I hadn't seen this bit before. They were talking about how things had changed between them. How they felt connected to each other again.

My glass filled up again as the image changed on the screen. The segment had ended, and it went back to the presenters. The female one was looking all doe eyed.

"Well, that was just lovely," she said. "What an incredible gift, to help people like that."

I felt a bit sniffly then. Lobster *was* a gift. She had changed the world around me so much in her short time here. For Andre and Divine, and for me.

The screen went silent. Callum had hit mute, I saw muzzily. I sat back on the sofa with a whump, my head spinning.

Lobster turned to look at me and raised her claws like a little hurrah. I heard myself laughing, from some distance away.

Callum and Sandy were grinning at me. Sandy was saying something about being proud, about how she was related to a star.

Callum topped my glass up again. I felt like everything was happening a long way away. We clinked glasses and I took another healthy swallow.

Was I famous now? My phone buzzed again, and Charlotte's

tweet made me chuckle.

She's a superstar and yet somehow still one of us. Congrats, Laura #bestfriend #dontforgetuswhenyougotohollywood #champagne later.

There was another text there too. From Dad. I didn't open it. I Liked Charlotte's tweet and put down the phone. Callum was talking. It sounded like a question.

"Sorry, what was that?"

"I asked if you'd seen Andre or Divine since?"

"No, I didn't even know they'd interviewed them. I mean it was just us in a room. Just like talking to some people in a cafe. I think a part of me didn't think it was really going to be on the TV until now."

Sandy raised a glass. "To the star."

We clinked again.

"Are you going to do it again?" she asked. "It was so good."

"I guess. I mean if they ask me."

"I can't believe you did it in the first place. You hate this kind of attention."

Lobster put her feelers up at me and then gently lowered them down to the table. I guess Sandy didn't mean that as it sounded.

"I thought I could help them," I said.

"You did. It's lovely. I'm so proud of you!"

I felt a warm glow settle into my stomach that probably wasn't just the champagne.

Sandy had to go after that. Places to be, people to see.

She hugged me goodbye and I saw her to the door. As it closed, I felt the room swim a little bit.

"Here," said Callum behind me. He was holding out the plate of pastries. "You haven't eaten yet."

"Thanks." I took a pan au chocolat and collapsed on the sofa.

"Coffee?" he asked.

"Yes, please."

The pastry tasted good and the smell of the coffee cut through my woozy head.

Callum put a cup of milky coffee down in front of me. "How are you feeling?"

"Fine." I took a big burny gulp.

"Was it strange seeing yourself on the TV?"

"Really weird. I felt like it was someone else. She looked happy and relaxed."

"She did. She was."

"Weird."

We ate another pastry each in silence. The breakfast TV continued silently on the screen. Smiling people mouthing words.

"I was on TV once," he said into the quiet.

"Really?"

"Yeah. A kids' TV show. When I was little. I was one of *The Secret Seven*."

I sat up and stared at him. "No!"

"Yep."

I remembered watching that as a kid. I squinted at him, but I couldn't remember any of their faces.

He raised his coffee cup at me. "Jack Trevelyan, at your service. We recorded one whole season when I was ten."

I grabbed my phone. "Is it on YouTube? Do you have a copy?"

"No, and no. I checked."

"Do you ever get recognised?"

"Once when I was about fifteen but not since then."

"Wow!" I took another pastry and sat back, amazed.

"So, if you want to do more of this you can," he said. "But if it makes you too uncomfortable you don't have to. You too can be someone who was once on TV for a bit. It's a good story to tell at parties."

We munched in silence for a bit. But it felt a bit less intense. He was right. I could do this as long as I wanted. I was helping people. It felt good.

Chapter Thirteen

Lobster was larger again than she had been. Where her legs had been drawing pins they were now matchsticks, where her claws had been cute, they were now mini-boxing gloves. Her visions were smoother too: mini stories and gentle nudges which told me everything I needed to know about people.

A mother dragging two children down the street, one of them held tight in the grips of a grizzly bear that was half-emerged from the cracks in the pavement. The boy was crying and struggling to get free. His mother, oblivious, tugged his hand and the child stumbled forward. The bear vanished beneath the stones to re-emerge from the next grout-line to catch at the child's legs. The child howled fit to burst. The mother stepped and yelled, "What is wrong with you?" The bear reared on its hind legs, emerging fully to tower over the quivering child. His sister looked on, wide-eyed, sucking her thumb.

The man across the road striding forcefully down the centre of the pavement. A cluster of half-real de-shirted hunks were behind him, all achingly good looking, strutting and jostling to push him out of pole position, each shove threatening to topple the precarious crown balanced on his beautifully waxed and teased hair. One of the hunks winked at me as they passed, another cocked a finger gun.

He passed a woman going the other way. She had to sidestep to prevent herself being flattened. She muttered to herself and carried on walking. Slight, pretty, head held high, she was the model of a busy professional. All smoothed hair and pencil skirt. Behind her on the pavement her shadow crawled with nightmares of tentacles, snarling maws, reaching fingers and mouths opened to scream. I caught the stench of it in the wind. When she paused to check her hair in a shop window the shadow reared up behind her like an empty wave. Ten, twelve feet of midnight nasties, threatening to crash down over her. I wanted to call out and warn her. Keep moving. Thankfully, she soon hurried on and the wave drew out as she strode forward, subsiding into an insidious trickle polluting the pavement behind her.

Another woman passed me, unburdened by children, or shadows, but walking braced and straight like a soldier. On her back was a silky backpack, grotesquely outsized. Through the bulging seams I could see paperwork, a babygrow, an iron, handmade bunting, and sexy lingerie. She was sweating blood under the weight of it.

All these people carrying their burdens. How did they bear it? For the first time I wondered, how did I not have one?

Chapter Fourteen

I started the new job on the Monday. As I approached the lego-building I adjusted the babygrow pantsuit and repeated to myself *this is the uniform, this will make me blend in.* I was already missing my hoodies.

The front desk felt so familiar. I walked amongst all the call-centre staff in their jeans and hoodies as they walked through the lobby with me and got into the same lift. Standing at the back behind the crowd, in the mirrored doors, you couldn't see my babygrow pantsuit and I could still almost think I was one of them. That's until the doors opened on the third floor and they all got out. The lift doors closed and I saw a professional-looking woman standing there with a shiny new handbag and a corporate hairstyle (thanks to Sandy's early morning visit).

That wasn't the only reason I was feeling pretty tired. Paula had had me in again on the Sunday. This time it was two school friends who seemed to be locked in a tangled battle over who was the most deserving of support. I watched them climbing over the piles of discarded problems like commandoes over battle-field corpses, standing on each other's hands, shoulders, and heads to be the most deserving, the most ignored. In the end, on top of their mountain of troubles, neither could even see the other anymore. It took some coaxing, and a lot of soothing of ruffled feathers – these two were chanticleers compared with Ciara – but eventually they quietened down. I got them talking about times they relied on each other and it wasn't long before they started opening up to the idea that they could do this better if they did it together.

I had maybe spoken to two or three people a week in my old life. Now it felt like legions.

The door opened on the fifth floor. Rashda was behind the desk and gave me a big smile. She called through to the office and said that someone called Rachel would be coming out to get me. I felt my pulse in my temples, matching the ticking of the shiny silver clock. Finally the door opened and a tiny bird-like woman walked out. Rashda leaned across and whispered, "Good luck."

Shadowing Rachel was a constant struggle to keep up. She was one of the most dedicated people I'd ever met. She was brusque as she walked me back to her desk. I found myself stumbling over my words.

As she showed me to my desk, I noticed something out of place. A rolodex, placed carefully on the edge, near the stapler. It span slowly, like a broken Catherine Wheel, the ticking of its pages like seconds of a clock. All the pages were blank. I opened my mouth to comment when it disappeared. Rachel was walking over to her desk nearby and as she reached it the Rolodex appeared next to her hand. Aha.

At lunch the next day, when I tried some of my standard small talk on her, she told me she never watched TV. Not even the news. When I'd asked what she did with her spare time she said she read industry journals, as if that were what everyone does on a Saturday night. She didn't know what a meme was but posted thoughtful industry posts to LinkedIn twice a day.

I didn't know what to say to that but then I thought of the empty Rolodex pages. All she had was her work; she didn't have many friends.

She started to open up after a few careful questions. She was lonely. She told me she had been on a reality dating show once where a group of people had a week of dinners together and each night voted one off the show.

"I was voted off on day one," she said. "Which I was a bit surprised about. But then when I watched the programme back, they said that they voted me off because I'd only ever talked about work." She shrugged.

We'd got on pretty well after that. In some ways we had a lot in common.

In my first client meeting with her I was surprised by how similar the script was from the calls I had been making downstairs. It reassured me.

"Good morning, thank you so much for making time for us today. How was the journey in? Not too long, I hope? Did the weather hold for you?"

"It's lovely out today. Almost too warm."

"Yes, it has been unseasonably hot hasn't it. I kind of wish we had air conditioning in this country. Do you want a window open? A coffee?"

Rapport. Rapport.

"No, I'm fine thanks."

"Well, let's get started. The reason we wanted to speak to you today was a new offering we've developed. I saw from your first quarter results that the young professionals' sector is proving to be

100

a big draw for you. Well, we have a number of connections with organisations targeting that sector that I'd love to tell you about."

I realised she had their attention when the client's sleeping dog in the corner lifted its head and started to watch.

I itched to slip my phone onto the table and hit record. Our scripts were similar but hers weren't written down. I wanted something I could play back again and again. Lobster seemed determined to stop me. She kept throwing images my way, distracting me from memorising the exact cadence, the right inflections.

At least Lobster was still useful in the TV show. I went back twice that week, in the evening for more shoots. Apparently, Paula said, they had got more audience engagement through my segment than anything they'd done in months. There was talk about a daily slot. We could shoot five sessions on the Sunday, she said, and spread them over the week, so it didn't interfere with work. If they needed reshoots I could do it in the evenings.

She showed me some of the comments. A woman in Wales said my insights had helped her in her marriage. A man in Somerset had reconnected with an old friend. A teenager in Hull had contacted her school counselling service. I was helping people.

At the end of a gruelling Thursday night shoot Paula met me in the Greenroom after recording. There always magically seemed to be wine after we recorded. This was my life now. Straight from work to the studio, then on to dinner with a tipsy Paula and a tipsy Lobster.

I stifled a yawn as Paula finished reading out the latest emails. I didn't want to look ungrateful and I was happy – just so, so tired.

"Do you mind if I ask you something," she said, pouring more champagne into my glass.

"Go ahead." The bubbles popped on my tongue.

"You said in recording, to that withdrawn woman, that you had picked up this skill only recently. That it could be learned."

I nodded. I had been echoing my conversation with Lillian.

"What did you mean? I thought you had always had this."

"No, not always. It was a gift."

"What do you mean?" Paula put down her glass of wine and leaned forward.

"It's something new that helped me see and understand people better."

"Something new? What, like a book, a class?"

Paula's got her interview head on, I grinned at Lobster. She understood even if I didn't say it out loud. We were sympatico. "Kind of. Like a coach, or a mentor, who helped me understand people. Helped me see their hopes and fears, what drives them."

"I get it, that makes sense. So, this coach talks you through it?"

I looked at her curious expression. Close enough. "Right."

"That's genius. So, you've been learning this skill as you go. Just recently? It's not an innate thing?"

I almost laughed. "No, definitely learned. And I'm not even sure I've done that yet. I'm still getting used to it. But I'm using her insights to guide me."

"I thought you were born with it. You said you were a sensitive child."

"My mum said so. But I don't remember that. I remember wishing I couldn't feel so much. I remember wishing I could shut it down. And then I remember wondering why I couldn't read people at all."

She was staring at me open mouthed. I ran that last bit back in my head. Had I said too much? It made me feel a bit itchy. But this was Paula.

She sat back. "But you said you were born like this. That means anyone can do what you do."

That didn't feel very nice to hear. "I guess so."

"You're not the one with the skill. You're just selling it."

I shifted in my seat a bit. How to explain? "I never said I was the…"

"How does it work? How often do you meet?"

"Well, it's not like a scheduled meeting. She's kind of just there."

She sat forward. "How?"

Why had I started this conversation? "It's hard to explain."

She was looking away, thinking. "When I saw you in the cafe you weren't with anyone. You just walked up to that girl."

Oh crap.

"So how was your coach guiding you?"

I tried not to look at Lobster. "It's hard to explain."

"Is it an earpiece?"

"No."

"Like a Bluetooth thing? Were you wearing it when we met for lunch?"

"No, I—"

"But you knew all about my mum, about my intentions. You called it out right there at the table. How did you do that? Was your coach there?"

"No. Well, yes. Sort of—"

"In the room? Was she listening in to our conversation?"

"I—"

She was leaning right across the table now, hands flat on the surface, glaring at me like a sphinx. I felt myself backing away. "Are you wearing an earpiece now?"

"No! I'm not. I'm not wearing anything. Look!" I pulled my hair back and showed her both ears. Lobster was on my shoulder, riding it out. *Help me out here*, I said silently.

Paula's expression didn't ease. "Just give me her number, I'll sort it all out. She'll get loads of business. She'll be happy, trust me." As she was leaning forward, I noticed something in her shirt pocket. It was shifting, like it was filling up with something. As she sat slightly straighter coins started falling out of her pocket into her lap.

I felt my head moving, shaking from side to side. I felt it filling up with hot water. There were no words.

Paula's expression was starting to darken. "Why not? Is it the TV show? You can keep your slot. I mean, you're ahead of the game. I won't dump you, I promise. Just give me her number."

I heard myself say, "I can't. Can we drop it, please?"

She sighed heavily and flung one hand up in the air. "Come on. Just be honest with me."

Lobster appeared in my peripheral vision, as if called out by name. She scurried a little way down my arm and looked up at me. She seemed to be saying, friends trust each other. They understand. I hoped she was right.

"I can't give you her number because she's a lobster."

There, I'd said it.

The face said, "I'm sorry, what?"

"My mentor is a lobster."

I looked up at Paula's face. Her face swam in my vision until it formed a blank sheet with features painted onto it. The expression was a kind one, a sad one, a shocked one, an angry

104

one. I couldn't tell any more.

The sides of the painted mouth turned down. "Yeah, you just had to say no." Her brows travelled across her face until they met with a crash that made me wince.

"She's here, in the room with us right now."

"What?"

I felt myself shrink in the searchlight emanating from the face.

"She's here. Right now. She's right there." I pointed at the table. Lobster put her claws up. Ta da!

The searchlight moved to the table and then back to me.

"Well, I mean, I'm the only one who... can... see..."

"For god's sake, Laura."

The face lurched upwards suddenly and resolved itself into an angry Paula, making me shrink back.

Paula's voice was loud. "Don't insult my intelligence. I thought you were a good person, but you're just a con artist."

The room sloshed slightly. A jolt that sent ripples out to the corners, that returned in interference patterns, throwing me one way and the other. Lobster ran back to my arm and clung onto my hand.

"I'm not," I yelled back. I took a steadying breath.

"This is bullshit." She pulled her coat off the back of the chair making the metal feet bang hard on the ground. She strode out of the room and closed the door behind her with a slam that rebounded off the insides of my skull.

I don't know how much time passed while I sat in that room feeling the vibrations.

I stood up. I put my coat on. I walked to the door. I walked down the corridor. I waved goodbye to the guard. I smiled, hard. I walked out into the street. I stopped at the kerb. I heard the crossing sound. I walked into the park. I sat down on a bench.

Then I was able to breathe. I gulped the air, hoping it would drive out the black pressure that had invaded me. Her face. Her voice. *What a load of crap. Don't insult my intelligence.*

No, that made me unable to breathe again.

Lobster crawled out of my hair and down onto my arm. Her feelers were stroking at the fabric of my coat, but I couldn't feel them. I couldn't feel anything, except shame. Deep, invasive, all encompassing shame.

I should go. I should go home. Get out of here.

It wasn't a surprise. It was never something that was going to work for long and I should be happy that I even got away with it at all. I mean, what did I think I was going to do here – help people? Become famous for helping people? Me?

I was the last person who would pull that off.

I stood up and started for home.

Walking was hard. That dark invasiveness all around me. Every step hurt. But the sensation of movement started to jolt something free. That little voice, the one that watched me. The tiny critic who told me what not to do.

I should go back to keeping my head down. It's only when I showed people my crazy that it hurt them. It's only when I let them see me that they judged me.

Stop all this nonsense about helping and just do what you do best. Be quiet, stop making waves, stop treading all over other people's lives.

The thoughts were helping. They seemed to pull the corset strings of my jelly existence tighter and tighter, forcing me back into a recognisable shape.

Do better. Be better.

I'll try.

I rounded the corner to my flat. How far had I walked? How long? There was a hole in my head where my brain should be. But this was a good thing. I felt nothing. The functioning, doing, part of my brain was gone.

I let myself into the house and carefully placed Lobster on the coffee table.

Out there was probably someone who was desperate for the chance to see these things. Someone who could make a good go of it. Who could help people.

I just needed a break. Just a little bit of time without all of this in my life. Just a few hours, a few days. She could stay in the room. I could come back for her. Just a week or two. Something.

She sat up on her haunches and her claws tapped together, a little staccato question. Maybe she could see all my thoughts before I could even form them. Maybe she knew what was coming. The thought made me feel even sicker.

"We need to talk," I said, then paused. Her feelers dropped. What was I saying – why had those words risen up automatically? Was I breaking up with her?

What words could I form to drive this sequence on, to push the world into the shape it needed to be? She had to let go of me and find someone else who would value her gift, who would value her.

"It's not you, it's me"; "I need some space"; "I need to work on myself"; "I'm not the person you think I am"; "You deserve better than me"; "It would be selfish of me to carry on"; "I have to let you go".

None of these were the right words. I had never learned the right words for breaking up with your lobster.

"I think you should go," is what came out of me, suddenly, like a pistol whip. Lobster's feelers dipped even lower, the tips flattening along the table.

"I can't have you hanging around anymore. It's too much for me."

She stepped her little feet towards me. I felt myself flinch away.

"No. You have to go. I can't."

She took another step and her feelers reached out towards me, to stroke my hand. I pulled it back sharply. My heart ached. But I couldn't do this any more. She had been wrong to pick me. I didn't need her help. It wouldn't work on me. I was already too far gone. She needed to just accept it and go. I wasn't going to change my mind.

"Please, just go. You're great, you are. Someone else would be happy to have you. But I can't do this."

She was flat against the table, now. Every muscle in her body loose and unresisting.

"No, stop it. Don't do that." She didn't move. Didn't she hear me? "Get up. Stop it. Don't play that game with me." Why was she just sitting there, so stupidly? My head started pounding. "It's not going to work. I'm not falling for this. I'm in charge here, not you, you little bitch."

I slammed my hand down on the table, millimetres from her inert little body. The force propelled her slightly into the air. She landed with a crunching sound that made me sick.

Then I saw him standing in the doorway.

Callum. Looking at me with wide eyes. I was insane, a psychopath.

Then I was sobbing and gasping like a child, sinking deep into a swamp of shame.

His arms settled around me. I clung to him. Huge waves of pressure rolling through me. His arms were steady around me as the waves receded.

As I came back to myself it dawned on me what I must look like. A crazy person shouting abuse at the coffee table, crying openly in public. The hotness of that thought was stronger even than the tears. I didn't want to look up or see his reaction.

Would I even be able to tell what his reaction was? He could be thinking anything about me – awful horrible things – and I would never know. His indifference had been so valuable. A safe, clutter-free space for me to come home to every day. Now it would be gone.

My eyes were squeezed shut by this point. I couldn't look at either of them.

Callum moved first. He pulled back from me, as he should, and put his hands on my shoulders. I leaned gratefully onto them, anticipating them vanishing – anticipating him vanishing.

"Hey," he said, a little jolt breaking open my eyes. "It's OK."

A totally unhelpful phrase. People said that at all kinds of times to mean pretty much anything. I searched his eyes, his mouth for clues. What did the crinkle on his forehead mean? What did the twist near his mouth signify?

"Let me get you a cup of tea," he said.

Of course, that's what you did for people who were distressed. He stood up and went over to the kitchen. I watched his back retreat. It was a reason not to look at the table quite yet.

How on earth could I explain what he had seen? The cup of tea was his payment towards normality, but I had no idea what my bill was. I should just thank him and go, then keep my distance for a while.

Maybe if I pretended this had never happened he would too and we could go back to watching Saturday night prime-time quizzes as normal.

I finally looked down. Lobster was sitting there. She took a step forward and one of her legs buckled. I cringed back from her accusing stare. I had hurt her, damaged her. My insides shrank away from the skin containing them, disgusted at being in contact with something capable of such violence.

When I reached out towards her, she raised her claws up and open, ready to bite. I put my head in my hands. Where had that anger come from? Why was I behaving this way?

But she would forgive me. She had to. She was my lobster, and I was her person. And people forgive their person, even if they hurt them, or reject them, or tell them they are making it all up. That's what makes them their person. I just had to give her some space, give her some time. I'd take her back to the room. Apologise. She'd know that I meant it.

Callum cleared his throat. He was standing by the sofa, two cups of tea in his hands. He handed one to me.

"Want to talk about it?" he asked.

Clearly, I owed him a response.

"I'm sorry for behaving like that," I said. Perhaps that would be enough.

He looked at me for a moment. I couldn't read the expression in his yes but his face wasn't squinched and angry. "It's OK," he said, eventually. "You don't have to talk about it if you don't want to."

"I don't want to," I said, gratefully.

"OK."

We sipped our tea together in silence. It was nice, sitting

there, silently staring into my mug.

"Thank you," I said, before I meant to.

"It's OK," he said and reached out and squeezed my hand where it lay like a dead fish on the sofa.

I should take Lobster to my room. Apologise, make sure she was OK.

When I looked at the coffee table Lobster was gone.

All the strength went out of me and I collapsed back in my seat.

Chapter Fifteen

When I walked into the tram station the next day the space was filled with people. Only people. The white noise of their footsteps fell like a salve on my ears. The tram announcements had the cadence of classical music. A single note held for a whole bar.

The tram was quiet, only the faint click of phone screens and the tutting of commuters; a very British silence. I closed my eyes and let my head rest against the glass, the welcome coldness settling into my skin. This was the right choice. It was better this way.

The journey felt long and short all at once. Walking to the office with no looming shapes or deafening racket, I may as well have been alone. The fifth floor seemed empty. Rachel waved me over as I came through the doors.

"Hope you've got your smiling muscles all warmed up," she said.

She handed me a business card. It was off-white, heavy, and textured. The inky-black words were chiselled into the paper.

"Who's Patrick?" I asked.

"He's the COO of that FMCG I told you about."

Everyone on the fifth floor spoke like this. That and neck scarves seemed to be the two main indicators of success.

I nodded to show willing. "When's the meeting?"

"In ten minutes." She shot me a look which appeared irritated.

Today, however, she seemed angry with me. I have no way of knowing why. She was typing something at her desk, and I wasn't sure what I was meant to be doing. Too little time to log on, too much to just stand there.

I went to the loo.

In the mirror the stylish suit buttons winked at me in the overhead lights. Mirror Laura was professional and ready. An interested expression and abundance of energy was all that was required.

I adjusted the resin necklace and repinned my hair. I looked the part. Now I had to learn the lines.

Rachel was standing by her desk when I got back. Her expression was tense, but I couldn't tell why.

"Come on," she said, unnecessarily.

We walked into the lobby. I smiled at Rashda behind the desk and she gave me a little thumbs up.

The meeting room corridor welcomed us politely. The boardroom was empty in a luxurious way. Rachel started checking the IT. I picked a chair and sat in it.

Rachel's attention to detail was legendary. For this meeting she had fifteen documents already open and ready to show on the screen but discreetly blanked. She even moved the room around to make it seem more welcoming; like Barry she was a stickler for rapport. When the potential customer walked in all they would see was hospitality and comfortable leather chairs.

The clock on the wall was the only thing making a sound – slight contrast to the last meeting where Rachel's rolodex was drowned out by the customer's circus clowns. I was supposed to watch and learn but the buckets of whitewash and exploding glitter cannons had made it hard to hear. Now I was rid of all that nonsense I might learn something.

The door opened and Rashda came in followed by the most handsome man I had ever seen. This must be Patrick.

Rachel sprang to her feet and advanced on him, hand extended. Their greeting was effusive but curiously guarded. I looked back and forth between them, two professional inscrutables.

"Thank you so much for coming, Patrick," Rachel said and showed him to a chair. "This is my colleague Laura who is sitting in with us today.

He came towards me, all smiles. His handshake was firm, a double shake and then a squeeze. It said that he was entirely in control. I would have to copy that one.

We settled around the table and Rachel began her spiel.

But this meeting with Patrick was the third one I'd shadowed and, the clown fiasco notwithstanding, I was beginning to recognise the flow.

She was word perfect. Really, an expert. When Patrick asked a difficult question she had the PDF on standby. He raised an objection and she shifted gears and matched it. It was a clockwork ballet. Given time I could learn it too.

Finally, the coffee was drunk, and the biscuits eaten. Patrick's expression didn't change until the final minutes of the meeting when he suddenly smiled, a beam that lit up the room, and slapped his hands on the table. He said he was won over and he wanted to sign.

"That's fantastic news," Rachel said and started to talk about the flow of signatories, but he said he was more of an immediate kind of person and wanted to sign the thing there and then. Rachel agreed warmly, clicked a button and left the room to get print-outs.

Once she was gone, taking her frenetic buzz with her, the energy in the room seemed a lot calmer. Patrick took another biscuit and sat back in his chair.

It could have been awkward, but I launched into my small talk repertoire. It was easy banter, back and forth, the kind I had honed at university parties, flitting from group to group.

Before long he had a twinkle in his eye that I recognised. It was nice. This handsome, successful guy was flirting with me. This was the stuff Tom had promoted me for, the stuff Dan had fallen for. Charming people I barely knew was my superpower. I didn't need any other.

By the time Rachel got back Patrick was leaning forward in his chair, laughing. Her arrival broke up the banter and they got onto the important business of signatures. Patrick shook our hands in turn. Two shakes and stillness, I met him movement for movement.

Did he hold my hand a little bit longer than before or had I imagined that?

Rachel led the way out into the corridor, clutching her precious paperwork to her chest. One small signature for Patrick, one giant leap for Rachel towards her hefty Christmas bonus.

Back in the lobby the small talk reached fever pitch. Promises of a lunch to discuss roll out. I told him our delivery team were going to become his new best friends which raised a laugh. It was a blatant copy of what Rachel had said to the dog man, but she didn't seem to mind.

He asked me for my business card. Rachel's surprise was a mirror of mine – I was an underling, a trainee. But it would have been rude to refuse so I handed it over. My flimsy colourful square was a poor attempt compared to his linen ivory masterpiece, but he seemed pleased to have it as he slipped it into his inside jacket pocket with a smile.

As the lift doors closed behind him Rachel gave me a nudge and laughed. She asked Rashda if she'd seen that and Rashda said she'd take bets on how long it would be before I got a call.

I felt a bit embarrassed, but they were nice about it.

Rachel said, "You can always go out for a few nice dinners and see. If you don't like him, you can lose his number. The contract's already signed." She nudged me again. "Maybe we both got a win today."

Sure enough, on the way home from work at six my work phone trilled and it was Patrick.

He didn't want me to feel conflicted, he said, by calling during work hours. I appreciated the sentiment, so I agreed to meet him for dinner on Saturday night. I hung up the phone feeling a bit smug. See, I didn't need an emotional support lobster. I was perfectly capable of running my life all by myself.

Back at the flat I came across Callum and his friend Craig playing noisy computer games in the livingroom.

"Hiya," said Callum. "How was the big sales pitch?" When had I told him? I hadn't even remembered it myself this morning.

"Hi. Hi, Craig." Craig raised a hand without looking up from the screen. "We won the bid. All signed and sealed."

"Congratulations. What's that, two out of three?" Callum put his controller on the coffee table and came over and watched me pour milk into a glass.

"Yup. Rachel says I'm her lucky rabbit's foot."

Craig piped up, eyes still on the screen. "Make sure she doesn't amputate it and hang it from a keyring."

Callum caught my eye and raised an eyebrow. I snorted with laughter.

"What?" said Craig. "It wasn't that funny." An explosion from onscreen signalled the demise of something or someone important and Craig threw a hand up into the air in despair. He waved the controller at Callum. "Mate, are you playing or what?"

Callum nodded and went back over to the game. The noise of it all, after weeks of spectral chaos, was too much so I said I'd take my milk into my room.

"Laura," said Callum before I reached the door. "We can turn this off?"

"No, I'm good. Thanks. I'm going to have a bath."

"OK. We'll turn it down a bit. Give you some peace."

"Thanks."

True to his word the gunfire dropped to a low rattle which was easily silenced by the bathroom door. My bath was silent and peaceful. Just me, a scented candle, and the blank checkerboard of white tiles.

Patrick sent me the name of a restaurant in the centre of town and I had looked it up on the internet – velvet drapes and industrial lighting – and realised I had nothing to wear to a place like that. Luckily, Charlotte was free.

"So," she said brightly. "Are we going to pick out your outfit?"

I opened up my wardrobe. The clothes Sandy had bought me were front and centre, sharp red and blues with cream and ivory. Clustered around the edges were the dark and floppy remnants of my old life. Well-worn jeans and baggy jumpers in shades of winter.

It wasn't long before we managed to find a skirt that could do for the evening. It was, not surprisingly, one of the ones Sandy had chosen for me. Transitional, I think she called it.

Tops were a different matter. Everything Sandy had picked out was a bit too corporate for a trendy night out and my old T-shirts just looked ridiculous. In the end Charlotte volunteered to go home and get a white satin blouse that she had for special occasions. Cleary, shopping trips and stylists, notwithstanding my wardrobe still mostly belonged to the old me.

I gave Charlotte my keys and she said she wouldn't be long, so I pulled on one of my oldest jumpers and went to make tea. It had oversized sleeves, fleece-lining in the front pocket and the word 'Meh' printed on the front.

As I walked down the corridor I caught sight of myself in the mirror, looking messed up and jumbled in my cat-paw slippers, Meh hoodie and tailored burgundy skirt.

I had some work to do before the evening.

The kettle was just boiling when the door went.

"In here," I yelled, thinking that she'd been quick.

But it was Callum who stuck his head around the kitchen door. "Afternoon," he said.

"Oh, hi. I'm making tea. Want one?"

"No, I'm good, thanks. Just changing for my run."

"OK, have fun."

He grimaced. "Let's just say I'll be glad when it's done." He indicated the window where raindrops were starting to fall.

"Oh. Yikes."

"Yeah. I'll be back in an hour or so."

"I won't be here. I'm going out."

I heard the door go again. Callum and Charlotte said hellos as she walked past him into the kitchen.

"I've the perfect top, posh restaurant be damned. Ooh, tea, thanks." She shook the raindrops off the plastic bag and pulled out a shiny white number. "A bit of lippy, stupid shoes, you'll knock his socks off."

Callum's eyes went from the top to my face and back again. "OK. Have fun." His head disappeared, then suddenly reappeared again. "Cool jumper."

"Thanks."

His head disappeared and, shortly after, the door shut in the hallway.

Never mind. I turned back to Charlotte. "Thank you." Meh this was not. "Help me pick out some shoes?"

"Of course. I brought some lippy too."

"Thank you."

She raised her cup of tea at me.

"No, I mean it. For everything."

"My pleasure. Have fun. Throw caution to the wind. Who knows, this could be good for you."

The restaurant was hushed and darkened, like going to tea at the headmaster's house.

I walked into the lobby and someone took my coat which was a shame because it was probably the best part of the outfit. I was shown into a bar area. Patrick was waiting for me and had already ordered us some aperitifs.

Something about the lighting or the thickness of the drapes meant that everyone was speaking in hushed voices. The murmur was soporific and when the menus arrived, I found

I had to move closer to Patrick just to hear the options. Not that it mattered because he ordered us both the tasting menu. Apparently, given who the chef was, it was the thing to do.

I hadn't been sure what we were going to say to each other, but Patrick was easy to talk to. The banter flowed like it had in the conference room.

He asked me how I enjoyed the dizzying heights of corporate sales.

"It's different," I said. "Not all of us are so used to the penthouse view and the expense accounts." He laughed at that.

He asked me about my interests, whether I had been to his favourite places, describing them to me with descriptions that made it feel like I was actually there smelling the sea air and tasting the crisp tang of the wine. Through it all he was watching me, like I was absolutely fascinating to him.

The waiter arrived then and showed us to our table. I tried to remember the last time someone had found me so interesting. Maybe Dan, right back in the beginning, before he started to find me closed and stand-offish. But even Dan had never watched me so intently, kept so much eye contact – and from such eyes. It was almost hypnotic.

I wished I could tell what Patrick was thinking. Sitting across the table from me, chin in his hand, asking me every question in the book.

When the tiny platters of food started to arrive, he asked the waiter questions about each one. His thirst for detail was unquenching. He seemed fascinated by the world around him, delighted by everything. He laughed with the waiter over a joke he had made.

Each dish was different, no two menus were the same, he

said, and he asked if I wanted to try his duck. I found myself leaning across the table, taking his fork into my mouth. It was as good as he said it would be.

When I went to the bathroom I paused, on the way back, took a moment for myself on the edge of the dining room and watched him. He was handsome from the front but from the side he had the most perfect profile. The kind you wanted to trace onto paper.

As I started forward he looked up and saw me. He had a lovely smile.

The evening flowed and it felt like a hundred years, and no time at all, before we were in the back of a taxi heading home.

By that point he was holding my hand. His thumb was gently stroking the back of my fingers, sending littles pops and fizzles up my arm. The taxi pulled up and the door unlocked.

How was the evening over already?

I turned to say thank you for a lovely evening but got caught in his gaze. I couldn't say a thing. He leaned forward and kissed me. A long, slow, closed-mouth kiss, like Clark Gable on the steps of Tara.

I was tempted then to say drive on, take me home with you. Make me feel special. I could see in his eyes that he wanted me to, but he was too much of a gentleman to say anything.

I kissed him again, chaste and simple – a touching of the lips – and opened the taxi door.

"Thank you for a wonderful evening," I said, one foot on the ground to keep me safe from temptation. "I hope we can do it again soon."

As the taxi pulled away, I saw him watching me through the back window and my heart skipped a little beat.

As I let myself into the downstairs front door I wondered

if Callum would still be up and whether it would be better if he was or wasn't. Charlotte would be ready, willing, and able for a full debrief in the morning and it would be fun to have someone to dissect the evening with, especially as it had all been a bit of a blur. But the thought of dissecting it with Callum made me feel itchy. Like talking about sex with your brother. No, not your brother, something else that felt strange and uncomfortable and really inappropriate. When the flat was dark and silent as I let myself in I breathed a sigh of relief.

Chapter Sixteen

The next day was a Sunday. I woke up late and groggy to the sound of tapping on the window. It was only for a moment, but I thought it was the tap, tapping of tiny pointed feet. Then I realised it was just raindrops.

I lay, befuddled, staring at the ceiling. Somewhere in the flat Callum was doing something noisy. There was banging then the water pipes groaned briefly. After a long pause I heard, faintly, music.

I could go out there and chat. He would ask me about my evening.

Or I could roll over and check my phone. Charlotte would be waiting by hers to hear a blow by blow. Or I could close my eyes and sleep some more before I had to get up for lunch with Sandy. Instead, my thoughts drifted to the rain. Did Lobster like it better when it was wet? She had liked the water in the sink so much. A tiny black figure, splashing and playing.

I finally climbed out of bed at 11am. The flat was quiet when I stuck my head out of my bedroom door, only the sound of the rain on the skylight in the hall. I padded down the corridor in my slippers and old dressing gown and made toast and tea.

What would Patrick say if he saw me like this? Ratty slippers and fraying towelette. It wasn't even a rhetorical question; I genuinely had no idea.

I went over the night before in my mind. It had been fun. Different. Enjoyable, certainly. When he had kissed me, it felt good. I tried to think back to old relationships. I must have also spent the early weeks wondering constantly what the other person was thinking. It just felt so alien after weeks of knowing. Lobster had thrown things into disarray and it needed some fixing. It would only be fair to give him a chance to fill in his own blanks.

Dan had been easier. We had liked the same things, hung out in the same places. He had tried so hard to get to know me. His sad expression came into my mind, asking me over and over again to just talk to him. I had never had any intention of sharing my inner life with him. That had been the cause of all of our problems. Of course, it had, how had I not seen it before?

Maybe this handsome man who was so at home in the world he inhabited, who didn't seem to want to delve inside her head, was just the thing instead.

My phone buzzed on the table, but I didn't pick it up. It could be one of only three people and I wasn't ready to talk to any of them yet.

I watched the trickles of rain on the windowpanes and reminded myself how lucky I was. I had a lovely flat, a shiny new job and a handsome new boyfriend. So what if my TV career was no more? Everything else was coming up roses.

Lunch with Sandy seemed to have become a habit. Sandy was late. That was becoming a habit too.

But I didn't mind. The cafe was full, but it seemed empty with only the people in it. After all the chaos and complexity Lobster had brought into my life, it was a relief to go back to normal. I had wondered if I would regret our parting, but life had simply continued.

Sandy came in all dressed in navy and red. She looked amazing, a burst of colour on a gloomy day. She gave me a hug and sat down.

"How did it go?" she asked. She unloaded her phone and wallet onto the table and shrugged out of her coat, somehow managing to drape it over the back of her chair without standing up again. She had on a tiny silver necklace, a cluster of chains or nets, something complicated.

She was staring at me. "So, your new job, how did it go?"

I realised I had been staring at the necklace to gather clues. How silly of me. "Fine. Good."

"What was it like?"

"It was great. I'm shadowing a woman called Rachel for now, going to all her meetings."

"What is she like? Is she nice?"

"She's very dedicated."

"Sound's terrifying."

"No, she's nice. She's a bit lonely so it makes her very focused on her job."

"Ah, yes, your magic insight." That gave me a jolt, but she carried on as if she hadn't just said something incredible. "What's your boss like?"

My brain was racing but my voice went on without it. "He think's he's god. Wears it like armour. Nary a chink."

Sandy was smiling. Had everyone noticed the change in me?

"You are so funny," said Sandy. "I think it's brilliant how you

125

can summarise people like that. It's such a talent."

I couldn't keep her eye. Not a talent anymore. But that didn't matter; I had all the information I needed from that brief adventure.

Luckily, the waiter came over. He dropped off the menus and water and left with an order for tea.

"How's your week been?" I asked quickly as she took a sip.

"The usual," she said. She put the water glass down and picked up the menu, turning it over in her hands. "Pretty much."

"That's good." I picked up my menu and scanned the soups, grateful for the reprieve. The potato and leek looked nice.

Sandy was still staring at the menu like the decision was too much to make. I worried that my avoidance had annoyed her, but she didn't look annoyed. She looked thoughtful.

The waiter arrived back at the table with the tea.

"The potato and leek soup, please," I said.

He nodded and tuned to Sandy. She didn't look up.

"Sandy," I said, making her jump.

"Sorry. The same."

The waiter took the menu from her hand. I gave the waiter a bright smile to fill the gap. He nodded and smiled back, barely glancing at Sandy before he left.

We sat like that for a minute, then she cleared her throat.

"Laura, I wanted to ask you something. It's personal."

"Yes, of course." Because this was our relationship now. Sisters who told each other personal things.

"It's about Alan."

"Lovely Alan. How is he? I haven't thanked him properly for that amazing scarf he got me for my birthday."

Sandy scowled at that. Was that the wrong thing to say?

126

Surely thanking someone for an expensive gift was correct. But she didn't say anything, she was just looking at her hands.

I plunged on. "I mean I'd heard abut cashmere being soft, but my god!" Still nothing. "He's so generous with that sort of thing."

Still no response. This wasn't working. I thought about Rachel and her technique of using silences to encourage someone to talk. I waited.

The waiter came back over and put down the soup, but she didn't pick up her spoon. She usually loved eating out. She loved fancy salads and things with quinoa and kale in them. She had even barely touched her tea.

OK, so she wasn't being like herself. Or rather, she was being like her old self, cold and distant. But not like the version of her after my promotion and the TV gig and she could finally be proud of me. Had someone told her that I had dropped out of the TV gig?

I opened my mouth to explain but, no. She was talking about Alan. Charming, chatty Alan. Always a twinkle in his eye, especially at his advertising firm. She was staring at her food without eating it. Oh dear. She had been so enthusiastic about my new skills. *She wants me to guess, to reassure her about the one thing she can't talk about.*

"Alan loves you, Sandy. He's not going to be worried about how much you weigh."

She looked up sharply. Her expression did not look relieved. But it had to be about this. Maybe I had phrased it wrong.

"I know he works with all those skinny waifs, but he loves you, just as you are."

Her mouth dropped open. I would have hoped in surprise at my ability to hit the nail on the head, but that was not an expression of awe. The warmth in her eyes started to fade.

"How much I weigh?" Her voice was cold.

"No! I'm not saying you have extra weight. I'm saying that even if you did, he still wouldn't look twice at any of those other girls."

She put her spoon down with a bang. "What other girls?"

"The ones... at work?" I heard my voice tail off into a squeak. "Honestly," I said, urgently. "You look amazing. So thin and beautiful. Trust me."

But it wasn't having the right effect. Her face was reforming into that look. A look I knew well, that had following me throughout my childhood, that she gave me every time I saw her. A look that I hadn't seen in months.

It was a curl of the lip, the accusation in the eyes. Of all the looks I could recognise, this was the clearest and the most familiar.

"I'm sorry," I said. "I've said something wrong. I didn't mean it. I was just thinking how good you look. Really thin. I like that dress."

She pushed her chair back from the table with a grating shriek. "How I look is not the only thing I care about, Laura."

I reached out my hand to her. "I'm sorry. You're right." She hesitated. I had to make her understand. "But it's the only thing you think about. If there's more things you care about just tell me. I want to know."

Before she left she leaned in closely and hissed, "Fuck's sake, Laura, sometimes you can be really cruel."

I walked away from the cafe with my head in a vice. What had just happened? Sandy was my friend. Except that now that friendship appeared to be a duvet over a bed of nails.

Underneath it I was still her weird sister who said the wrong things all the time.

I stumbled down the empty street. All my relationships were a knife-edge balance of saying and doing the right thing all the time. Step the wrong way once and you're off the board.

I rebounded off a person because a part of me assumed he would be imaginary. I guess, in a way he was. All of them were. Impossible riddles that only a supernatural lobster knew the answer to.

I found a bench in a quiet square, mind empty. Why hadn't she just left me alone – clueless and never knowing what I was missing? Why would she come and tempt me and then leave me feeling all empty and isolated? I had been doing just fine before.

Across the square there was a flurry of activity. Someone had sat down at the opposite bench and the entire square's worth of pigeons took to their wings to settle around him, cocking their heads in case he had any crumbs he could throw down to brighten their day. My side of the square was empty, as if there were nobody there at all. My heart thumped painfully in my chest.

I wasn't fine before.

The sentence appeared in my mind for the first time in my life. But it had the familiarity of an old friend, like the mouse that lives under the skirting board, rarely seen but constantly leaving around the place little reminders of how squalid the place was.

I watched the thought warily for a while, offered it some cheese.

Was this my spectre? Was this what Lobster saw when she looked at me? A mouse, hiding away from everyone and everything, wondering why I felt invisible.

Chapter Seventeen

The silence was starting to become unnerving. After weeks of seeing all their inner workings exposed for my prying eyes their blank faces, locked up like safes, not a sound emerging, were almost shocking. A world of monochrome. Hushed, bare, empty.

Back to normal.

Lillian was proving to be more difficult. I had managed to avoid her so far – I told Carol to tell her I was diseased, and I folded clothes contentedly for four hours. But when I came back the following Saturday she was waiting for me in the hall.

"Hi Lillian," I said brightly, stopping near her chair but just far enough away to make it clear that I wasn't staying to chat.

"I have tea," said Lillian.

Clive was watching with interest from behind the desk. "Great! That's good."

She was holding two cups of tea, with her cane hanging from one wrist, shuffling across the floor unsteadily. How she got the door open as well, I'll never know. It was a choice between letting her fall over in the middle of the floor, tea and all, or stepping in and engaging. There were already sloshes threatening to overwhelm the cups, so step in it was.

I took the cups and she made good use of her cane, making it across the hall to the Day Lounge much faster than expected with it bearing her weight. Clive was smiling at me so I followed her in. Sneaky.

She nodded over to the side of the room where our cabinet sat, flanked by two of the orthopaedic chairs. Right, she needed something comfortable to sit on. I was being thoughtless.

I put her cup onto one of the coasters that had appeared. It had a llama on it. She picked up her tea from where I had put it and took a noisy sip. I watched the steam curl around her nostrils like mist over a mountain.

"So," she said. "What's wrong?"

I picked up my tea. It was burning hot. How was Lillian drinking this? She must be like asbestos.

"Nothing." I hadn't meant to sound like such a teenager.

Maybe that's why she said, "I have four kids of my own and two of them were very good at hiding their feelings. The other two you couldn't have stopped from telling you any more than you could stop a dog from drooling. You're not one of the droolers."

Lovely imagery. "No," I said.

"Doesn't mean I can't read you. Just like my Amy."

I glared at her shoulder. Surely, she must have her own lobster. Not that I could see even if she did. I could hear her gentle breathing in the chair next to me. I could see her hands resting on her cane. But that was all. Lobster would have made me talk to her but then Lobster had ruined my life.

I should be enjoying the lack of ghosts and graveyard breaths. I should be feeling just how much I had my old life back. Sitting in a room full of people who were all blessed with the privacy and sanctity of their own minds. Instead the quiet of the lounge was working some other charm. What was the harm of talking into this empty space?

"I think I've made a terrible mistake," I said. Was that what I had meant to say?

She didn't respond but the chairs seemed interested, so I carried on.

"I broke up with my... friend." Would they notice the pause? Would they think I was being coy about a beau? "And now she's left, and I miss her."

"What happened?"

"Being friends with her brought up some things."

"Hmmm."

Clive was back at the reception desk. Someone had arrived and was talking to him; I could see his hair bobbing animatedly through the corner of the glass doors. Him and his phoenix. I'd never know what that meant now.

"What are you going to do?"

She was looking right at me when I turned. Her expression was direct but unreadable. Why were people so damn hard to understand?

"I don't know. I have no idea where she has gone. I said some horrible things."

"What things?"

"Oh, that I wish I'd never met her, that she ruined my life, stuff like that."

"No, I mean what things did she bring up?"

The words came out of my mouth without touching my brain to check if they were correct. "She tried to get me to see that other people have insides that I never knew about. She encouraged me to tell people what my insides were like." Huh, what did that mean?

"And what happens when you do. Does the world end?"

An image came into my mind. An image from the back recesses of my mind. My father, with a suitcase in his hand, standing in the doorway. My mother's hand on my shoulder.

"Yes," I said.

Lillian nodded but didn't say anything in particular. The silence made me wonder. Had it been so bad? I liked being more than just related to Sandy. I liked knowing Evan recognised me, even when he pretended not to. I liked seeing Charlotte helping herself. I missed knowing these things. Yes, there had been some bad, but now what did I have?

"So, what are you going to do about your friend?" Lillian said.

"I think I need to get her back."

I went out walking the streets in the late evening. It was grey and drizzly outside, but I didn't care. I guess I hoped that being out there looking would be enough to signal to her: I've changed, I'm ready to welcome you back.

I just wanted my lobster. Without her, everywhere I looked was exactly the same. All the people looked exactly the same with their lidded eyes, hunched shoulders and shrouded feelings. I'd had a hope of connecting with them, because I was really seeing them for the first time in my life, and now that was gone. The world was a lighter, brighter, much busier and more interesting place with her in it and I messed it up. Just like I always did.

How did you bring back your imaginary pet? How did you advertise that she was lost?

Except that she wasn't lost. She left, by her own choice.

134

I let myself back into the flat. The water had managed to seep its way through my supposedly waterproof coat. My armpits were wet.

I hung the soggy lumpen thing above the bath and put the kettle on.

My hair was damp on my head. I rubbed it with a towel and changed into comfy leggings and my 'Meh' hoodie.

The cup of tea pushed the coldness out of my body. I sat on the sofa and stared out of the window. There was something about a drizzly night that I could usually watch for hours, settled on the sofa in the warmth of that little flat; cocooned inside its cosy warmth while the weather did its best to insinuate itself inside. A certain smugness.

That feeling was missing tonight.

A quiet but insistent tap, tap, started up somewhere from the depths of the flat. Something dripping.

At first it was soothing but the endlessness of it started to get on my nerves. Maybe because it echoed with the rain outside. Maybe, some of it was getting in.

I went to investigate. Not the kitchen or the loo. Not my bedroom. It was coming from the bathroom. Of course, my coat.

As I walked into the room I reached for the bathmat, intending to put it under the dripping coat and make it quiet.

The coat was there, the drips were there, but as well, underneath, her back to me, dancing in the intermittent waterfall, was Lobster. She was reaching up her claws to try and catch the drips as they fell.

Lobster!

Her happy dancing was contagious. I must have made a noise because she turned to look at me. She ran towards me, down the length of the bath, claws outstretched.

I fell to my knees and put my hand out to her, and she ran on without a pause. The pin pricks felt like music on my hand, a little heavier, a little slower than before.

My lobster was back.

Her tail was up, and she danced a little jig. As she danced, I saw all six legs. They were all there. She was moulted and healed, like nothing had happened at all. I wanted to kiss her, hug her, yell, and sing.

Then the strangest thing happened. Lobster pushed herself up onto her feet, poised like a ballerina on the tips of her toes. She tensed and pushed herself gently and suddenly up into the air where she hovered, as if floating.

She drifted a little, weaving from side to side inside the bathtub. She gave a little kick of her legs – a thrill, like fingers over harp strings – and she moved up and out of the bath before drifting down towards my lap.

I jerked slightly as she landed. She ran her feelers across the top of my thigh. It was a gentle touch, one of her affectionate strokes.

My heart leapt. She was forgiving me. After what I had done, what I had said. I reached out with a shaky hand and she hopped on.

I hadn't broken her.

She gave a little squeak. It sounded happy. Then she bunched her legs and sprang.

She was flying, floating, turning somersaults in mid-air. Backwards and forwards, her feelers flailing, her tail flicking into a curl. She seemed so pleased. She was super-lobster. Faster than a speeding crustacean.

I heard myself giggle. Lobster paddled through the air

136

towards me landing elegantly on my shoulder. I let her reassuring weight arrive. She was so much bigger.

I took Lobster through into the bedroom and set her down on her old space on the bedside cabinet. She did two little turns and then settled, watching me.

We stayed like that for a while. I took in her beautiful blue lustre, the shininess of her shell.

I reached out a finger and she allowed me to gently run it along the newly healed leg. Guilt twisted in my chest. But Lobster reached down with her feeler and ran it over the back of my hand.

I watched as she grew sleepier, her feelers eventually settling along the tabletop.

It was 1am, the next time I checked the clock. I had been staring at her for hours. Just simply worried that she might not still be there if I closed my eyes for too long.

I had expected her to punish me for what I had done. But she wasn't. I wanted her back and she came. Did I deserve such kindness? I decided then that I would earn it. I would respect her wishes and together we were going to make the world a better place.

This was it. This was the secret. Why Lobster had come to me. I was right about it being a super power, but it wasn't there to help me be a better daughter or a better friend. That's not the kind of thing superpowers are for. Superpowers exist to make the world a better place. I had been selfish, that's why it had gone wrong. I had given up on the first try. I had to try again.

But what to do? I just had to keep my eyes open.

Chapter Eighteen

Sandy had become a ghost. She wouldn't return my texts or calls.

Clearly, I had got it wrong, but she was my sister. Sisters got things wrong all the time and they were still sisters. Or they should be.

Luckily, we were both going to Mum's for lunch. I could smooth things over, apologise for whatever it was I had done. I had a script all prepared but there was no guarantee she would accept it. I had a back-up as well just in case. One of them would work surely.

Mum led the way into the sitting room when she broke the news. Sandy wasn't coming.

Damn.

"What's up with you two?"

"Oh nothing. I said the wrong thing and now she won't let me apologise."

"Oh well, you know Sandy. I'm in her bad books too. She likes to hold a grudge."

"She does?"

Mum was nodding. "She's still mad at your Aunt Cathy for

throwing out that old backpack."

"What backpack?"

"You remember. She used to carry about some horrible tatty canvas army thing."

"The one with all the badges that she made?"

"That's the one. It was disgusting and filthy, but she was devoted to it."

"So why did Cathy throw it out?"

"Because it was disgusting. She couldn't go off to her new school with something like that. What would everyone think? But there was nothing at all I could say. You know what she's like. Stubborn. So, Cathy took the hit for me and boom, it was gone."

Sandy, that last day before leaving for boarding school. The slammed doors, the crying. The goodbye note I had left her that I had found kicked under the bed. Refusing to say goodbye to Mum and Cathy the next day. Refusing to say goodbye to me.

"So that's why she doesn't like Cathy. Maybe it wasn't such a good idea in the end."

Mum snorted. "You have no idea. Cathy was a godsend. It's hard being a solo parent, no-one else to be the bad guy. Sometimes it was nice to have someone else there to do the dirty work."

"Didn't Cathy mind?"

"No. She's got skin as thick as a rhino. Nothing gets through that. It was necessary, you know. You remember that horrible thing."

Barely. Khaki, a bit frayed. Kind of stinky. "Right. Of course. Maybe it was just really important to her," I tried.

"Laura, for god's sake. I'm taking your side here."

"Of course. Sorry. Thank you."

She muttered to herself. "Both of you constantly picking fights."

I looked up surprised. The house had been so silent. "Both of us?"

"Don't you remember all that trouble with the school? She got in with the wrong crowd. There was smoking and staying out 'til all hours."

"Sandy did?"

"Thankfully, the school were really good about it and we sorted it out quickly. Cathy helped me with that one too. That's when we had to send her off to boarding school."

"I never knew that was why. I thought she wanted to go."

Mum snorted again and took another gulp of wine. "You see. You thought you were the only one with a past. You were difficult early, all the stories and invisible friends causing problems, but it was Sandy who was the troubled teen. In some ways I think she has never gotten over it. She regresses every now and again. Stubborn."

Mum went off into the kitchen to fetch the food. I watched her retreating back. Sandy, the golden child, the goddess, was a problem child? I tried to imagine back to how things had been, but it was all a blank. All except Mum being upset all the time.

She came back through from the kitchen. No wonder she had a gnome and a will of iron. All this time I thought I had been the only one. "Sorry we were such a handful."

"Oh, it's water under the bridge. Children are meant to stress their mother out. It's part of the process. Don't worry, it'll be my turn next, when I'm old and batty. You'll find me out on the streets in the altogether."

I snorted at the thought. "I can't imagine that."

"Well, neither can I but life has a funny was of giving you lemons."

I tried to imagine my mum doing anything that wasn't entirely correct. It was impossible.

"Never mind. That's years off yet. You can cross that bridge when we find me naked under it."

I laughed politely.

"Tell me all about this new job then. I've been boasting about how successful you are."

"Oh, it's great. Bit scary, but the people are nice. It's not so different than the last one."

"But you're meeting all sorts of interesting people? CEOs and the like?"

"I am, yes. I actually met someone nice."

"You did? Who?"

"His name's Patrick. He's the CEO of a company we work with. We went out on a date last weekend."

"Didn't I say you should go for it? I'm really proud of you."

I felt my cheeks flush. "Thank you."

"Will you be seeing him again?"

"We have a date tonight."

"We should have a celebration of all the progress you've made." She got up and went to the fridge. "Look I got this in specially."

She brought two individual bottles of Prosecco, tops already unscrewed, and two flutes back to the table. We poured them out and touched glasses with a little clink. "To my clever daughter. It's so nice not to have to worry about one of my children. Do you have business cards? Can I have one. I want to show Cathy."

I left the house after dark, my head spinning. Years of sitting at that table feeling awkward. Surplus to requirements. Watching Sandy and my mum laughing and trading friendly insults. And behind it all Sandy was the troubled daughter?

Was that why Sandy was so worried about how she came across, was she trying to impress Mum? Make up for all the trouble she had caused? Was I the stable one after all?

Chapter Nineteen

That night was my third date with Patrick. I got ready with Lobster sitting on top of my chest of drawers. I showed her outfit after outfit. She didn't comment of course but even talking it through out loud helped.

"Nope. This top is not working at all." I threw it onto the bed, on top of the enormous pile of rejects.

I was nervous. It had been such a great two dates, but I hadn't had Lobster with me. What might I learn now that I did? I thought back to the couple in the park, the silver filigree threads tying them together. What if they were there between Patrick and me? What if they weren't?

I tried on a black T-shirt. It was plain but the fabric was nice, satiny, and there was pretty stitching on the edging. It was an old favourite. Smart enough for most places but not too stuffy. It was familiar, like an old friend. I could use an old friend tonight.

"Yes, that works," I said to Lobster. She cocked her feelers at me. Whatever that meant.

The T-shirt felt great on. I topped it off with skinny black trousers and heels. I didn't have a bag that would look right but I could just put everything in my coat pockets. The me in the mirror looked like someone halfway between the old and the new me. Well, he had to find out sometime. I added some lipstick to compensate. There, that would do.

Lobster leapt up into the air – it still made me jump – and followed me towards the hall. Callum was walking past the door when I opened it.

"Very nice," he said.

"Thank you."

He looked past me into the room. "Hard time choosing?"

I shrugged and fell into step beside him. "Yeah, he keeps taking me to these ridiculously expensive places."

"And you're running short on Armani?"

I smirked. "Yeah, this season's anyway."

He laughed. "Well, you look great. If he likes you, he won't care about what you're wearing."

I thought of Patrick's designer tie pin and shiny shiny shoes. I wasn't entirely sure this was true. Callum was wearing his battered old-man slippers and jogging bottoms. "You not going out then?"

"No," he said. "Quiet night in. Popcorn, movie. Pizza, maybe."

As if in response the wind howled around the edge of the building.

"Sounds cosy."

"Well, if you will insist on having a life," he grinned.

The window rattled. I could see clear bright stars over the tops of the buildings. I could already feel the cold.

Callum sat down on the sofa. The warm inviting sofa. "You can take my scarf if you want," he said.

"Sorry?"

"The blue one. It's really warm." He pointed to where it was hanging, right next door to Alan's cashmere gift – which was smarter, and went with the outfit better.

"OK, thanks."

"Have fun."

"Thanks."

I closed the door behind me and wrapped the blue scarf tightly around my neck. He was right, it was warm.

As I walked to the Tube, the wind whipped and danced around my ankles. It didn't bother Lobster at all, who bobbed along beside me without a care. Cheater. The street was filled with people, heads down, hurrying past me. With my eyes half closed I could only see their shrouded forms, unable to tell the real from the spectral.

It was comforting, having them back. But annoying too. A quiet cafe was never quiet. Even a half-empty Tube was abuzz with things that slimed and stank and sang.

As we left the Tube station, the wind plucked at my feet again. Along the pavement, the restaurant finally arrived, all glass and steel. Stepping through the door made me stumble as the wind loosened its grip.

I caught sight of myself in the mirrored lift walls and hastily stuffed the blue scarf in my bag. My hair was all over the place so I did my best. By the time the doors opened at the top floor I thought I looked suitable again.

The lobby was an odd shape, with a flight of stairs up from the lift and a podium at the top. There was no host at the podium.

I looked around. The tables were off to the left behind tall planters filled with ferns and monstera.

Through the broad leaves I caught sight of the back of

Patrick's head. The precise cut of his hair at the nape of his neck was unmistakeable.

I stepped close to the palms and called Lobster close. Was that a glint of silver I saw around him?

As I was squinting as the waitress came over to his table. He turned to talk to her, and I took in the perfect curves of his face. A profile that took my breath away. The waitress was clearly smitten too. She was flirting with him; hip cocked, head on one side. Everyone was so immediately charmed by him. He had such a gift.

Lobster finally came into range. The waitress had a cat curled around her neck. It was apparently asleep. As she laughed at something Patrick said the cat opened one eye, looked over at him and yawned. Not so interested, after all.

Patrick, however, was clearly enjoying the attention. I looked closer at him but there was no spectre at all. Just him, sitting poised and beautiful and receiving fake flirting with his particular grace.

Nothing scary hovered around him. No slimy beast or noxious fumes. He was exactly what he presented to the world. Charming and good.

My nerves and fears subsided, and I stood there, grinning like an idiot.

"Ma'am?"

I turned to see the host was back.

"Hi," I said, backing away from the plants. "I'm here to meet Patrick Keeler." The host nodded and smiled. "He's over there," I added helpfully.

"Of course, may I take your coat?"

"Thank you."

I shrugged out of it and he walked away. Back at the table

Patrick reached out towards the waitress' hand. What was happening? The waitress drew back sharply.

Her shoulder cat sat up suddenly and hissed. Patrick's expression changed into a scowl. Something bloomed under his suit, twisting inside his jacket. My gut twisted instinctively in response.

The waitress turned to go, oblivious, rolling her eyes as she did so. Once her back was turned another Patrick erupted from his chest. A dark shape, all angles, hands outstretched. It grabbed at the cat, but the animal leapt for safety. I thought the cat was clear, but the monster had it around its throat. The cat fought and spat as it twisted in his hands.

"Ma'am?" The host was in front of me. I could barely hear him through the pounding in my ears. "It's this way." He turned, expecting me to follow him.

I heard my breath in my ears. Where was the waitress? Was she OK? I searched the room and spotted her over by the bar. The cat was safe on her shoulders. Back at his table, Patrick's spectre throttled its imagined, helpless victim.

I had to leave. But my coat, with my keys and phone in the pocket. Perhaps I could get the host to get it without Patrick seeing. I stepped forward to catch his retreating back.

Then Patrick's head turned, and he looked straight at me. Instantly the monster and the yowling cat disappeared. He waved one hand and stood.

"Laura," he said.

The host was already at the table. I had no choice. Lobster landed lightly on my shoulder and retreated to the back of my neck. I could feel little tugs and twists as she buried herself into my hair, safely. It was only me who was exposed.

"Hi," Patrick said, standing up. He leaned in to kiss my cheek.

I held myself rigid and plastered on a smile when he sat back down.

The host pulled out my chair. I stared at him. He stared at me. I looked at Patrick. He raised an eyebrow. Reluctantly I sat down. The host asked me if I knew what I would like to drink.

"Um." I slid awkwardly into my seat.

"I've heard the martinis here are excellent," said Patrick, and nodded at me, his eyes sparkling with warmth.

The host turned to me and I nodded, mutely.

"So," Patrick's voice brought my attention back to him. "How has your day been?"

I felt Lobster rustling about at the nape of my neck. I was here now. With the firm's top client. A simple dinner. Small talk. Then an early night. No problem.

It was just a spectre.

"It was busy," I said, as smoothly as I could. "Business is booming. You know what it's like."

"I do indeed," he said.

"Better than being bored." I laughed lightly and he joined in. "How was the art show you were telling me about? Did you go in the end?"

A waiter appeared with my drink, interrupting us. As he introduced himself and started talking about the specials I looked over at the bar and saw the waitress watching us.

A menu appeared in front of of me and I clutched at it.

"Shall I order for us?" Patrick asked.

I looked back at him and his smooth smile and heard myself say, "No, thanks."

His lip curled. Except that it didn't. His actual face was a calm and measured as always, a slightly charming smile hovering at the corner. The lip curl was only visible to me, layered on top like a hologram. I tried not to recoil.

"I'll have the gnocchi, please," I said.

"No starter? My treat."

"No, thanks."

His eye twitched. I shouldn't be baiting him. I should be waiting this out charmingly. But now I was settled in for the meal the memory of the cat writhing in his monster's hands was making me unexpectedly angry. I watched his face as he finished ordering his meal, no starter, and he was barely giving anything away.

"What were we talking about?" he asked, disarmingly.

"The art show," I said bluntly.

He quickly got back into his stride. The art show was a riot of colour and characters, all of them described to me with just the right balance of generosity and gentle mocking to make him seem clever and observant in comparison. How observant he was, how unbamboozled by the shows put on by those around him.

I listened with interest, less about what he was saying and more about the way he was saying it. The script was almost entirely correct. The same comments you would hear from anyone about their busy social life. Except that every now and again there was a twitch in his eye, a curl of the lip.

Like then, as he was describing a lawyer who was holding court in the gallery, telling everyone what they already knew.

"She was quite the expert," he said and we both smiled in acknowledgement. But his smile, open and charming on the surface, contained a spectral toothy sneer.

I had taken him at face value. He was so smooth and charming. So good at making people feel seen. Making me feel seen. The waitress hadn't been fooled for a minute. I looked across. She was still standing at the bar, watching us. When she saw me looking she gave a wan smile and turned back to stacking napkins. She was talking to a waiter who I hadn't seen before. He was looking across at us and nodding.

When they were watching us, what did she see? Two charming people talking about everyday life. Laughter and witty repartee. One of them cold on the inside.

Or was it two?

Patrick was looking at me expectantly.

I was supposed to be answering something. "Sorry, what?"

"I asked whether you had seen the *Panorama* report last night."

"Oh, no, I missed it. What was it about?"

"Corruption in the government. Ministers awarding public contracts to their friends."

"Ah. No, I didn't see it."

"It was horrifying."

I pushed my gnocchi away, half eaten. "Right, yes. Awful."

"I mean what kind of person does that?"

I felt Lobster's claws tighten in my hair. His words were so reasonable. His eyes were filled with concern and empathy but his horrible shadow was laughing and laughing and laughing.

I opened my mouth to say something but the waiter appeared at the table. "Everything OK here?"

Patrick twisted in his seat and looked over at the bar. "What happened to our waitress?"

"She went off shift, sir."

Patrick sighed, a big angry sound. "Fine." It came out like a bark. "We're fine."

The waiter nodded and walked away.

But Patrick turned back to me. His smile was the same as it was before. But his shadow self was watching the waiter's retreating back and I saw it mouth the word *bitch*.

I found myself up on my feet. "I have to go," I said.

"What? Why?"

"I'm leaving."

"What the hell is wrong with you?" He looked horrified. I saw I had slammed my hand down on the table. A wine glass had fallen over and the red liquid crept across the table like a pool of blood. The restaurant had gone silent. Everyone was staring.

"I can see what you are," I said. "I can see what you think about, what you enjoy doing, and you are not as clever at hiding it as you think you are."

His expression was a picture of innocence as he looked around at the audience, hands raised in puzzlement. But I wasn't talking to him anymore. I was talking to his other half who was looking frightened. "Stop pretending!" I hadn't realised how loud I had said it until the waitress started walking towards us. I thought she was going to throw us out, but she was holding my coat and bag.

I took the cue and walked away from the table. She met me halfway and handed my things across.

"You OK?" she asked.

"Yeah. I think so," I said. Something occurred to me. "I'm so going to get fired."

From behind me I heard Patrick say, "Come back and talk about this, like adults."

The waitress squeezed my arm and I walked on without looking back.

Then I heard him roar my name. I ran down the stairs and

151

stabbed at the lift button. The top of the stairs was too close, too open. I clutched Lobster to me. There was nowhere to hide in this shiny, marble lobby. I had never felt so exposed in my life.

A ping.

Finally, the doors trundled open and I was inside punching the buttons.

The lift doors slid ponderously, achingly, closed.

Only then did I breathe out. Lobster was clinging to my chest. She seemed horrified and relieved in equal measure.

What the actual hell?

He'd seemed so nice, so charming.

The doors pinged open into a gloriously empty lobby. We made for the door, my stupid heels clicking and slithering on the marble.

When I was safe on the Tube, I finally let Lobster go. I kept my head down, ignoring all the noise, and let my shoulders relax. Deep breaths. A horrible man but just a man nonetheless. I was safe.

I let my head fall back against the Tube window. How could I have missed it? Months of finding out I was misjudging people, assuming them to be cold when they were a riot of colour and spectacle. And then this. Thank god for Lobster.

Was I wrong about everyone? How many times in my life had I taken the wrong path? Made the wrong choice? Trusted the wrong person. It felt like everything was in flux, tumbling around in a washing machine. It was not pleasant.

Work was going to be interesting. Tom would probably be mad at me for dumping his best client. A hundred different stressful conversations crowded into my mind. But as I watched Lobster shake off the tension by doing backflips in the carriage aisle, I thought none of them would be worse than staying on that date.

I rummaged in my bag for my back-up flats and pulled off the painful high heels, putting them onto the seat next to me. The blue scarf came out with the second ballet pump. I wrapped it around my neck. Repercussions were a problem for tomorrow. For now, a night in with a pizza, popcorn and a movie sounded good.

When I walked through the door Callum looked like he hadn't moved a muscle all night. The only difference was a half-empty pizza box. I was immediately envious. The sofa was calling me.

"Hey," he said. "You're back early. Everything OK?"

How to answer that one? I dropped onto the sofa next to him.

"Bad date?" he asked.

"You could say that, yes." I felt a little wave of something sour in my stomach and sighed heavily to get rid of it.

Callum sat forward and pushed the pizza box along the coffee table. "Beer?"

"Yes, please." The pizza smelled good and I picked up a slice. It helped settle my stomach.

"So, what happened?" Callum handed me an open beer bottle and slumped down next to me.

I took a big gulp. "Turns out Patrick is not who I thought he was."

"Not good?"

"Not good."

"Sorry."

I looked across at him. He did seem genuinely sorry. For

some reason I had thought he might be pleased.

He raised his beer bottle. "To someone better."

"I'll drink to that." We clinked.

"What are we watching?"

"*Die Hard.*"

I pulled a face.

He laughed. "I like it. The good guys win."

"Tough day at work?"

"Yeah. Not enough good guys won."

"Not as simple as blowing them up?"

He snorted. "I wish. They're too convincing and clever. They get away with it because they look the part. It sucks."

Like Patrick. He was probably still sitting in his expensive restaurant getting away with being just horrible while to the rest of the world he was charming, successful, and perfect. Bad guys dressed as good guys.

Maybe that was what I could fix. "Imagine if you could show people what these guys were really like, under the charm and money," I said.

He gave me side-eye but said, "Yeah, that would be great."

"Who would you show?"

"Me? Well, the judge would be a good place to start."

"Why?"

"Well, the arguments they use in court are basically, did the person do something legally wrong? Yes: go to jail or get fined. No: you're free to go. And they sometimes take account of circumstances but not often. Eighty per cent of people in prison have some kind of mental illness. Sixty per cent are from poor backgrounds. Seventy per cent are men. We do not handle distress well in our society."

"That's awful." I had been thinking about unmasking the bad

guys and he went straight to showing people the good they were missing.

"Yeah, but thinking about it, the Director of Public Prosecutions would be better. Someone with a lot of power. Someone who could actually change things."

The adverts finished and the news came on. Callum always watched the news. He was interested in what was going on in the world. I never had been until now. I would go and make supper or read in my room, come back out for the late-night talk shows. This time, I stayed and watched.

Callum was patient. He answered my questions about how all these strangers made up the fabric of the system. Why weren't these people doing a better job?

"It's the best we've got," Callum said.

"But they're just working to their own interest instead of helping other people."

Callum turned to look at me. "It's nothing new. It's always been this way. I think people try their best, but the system is a hard thing to turn."

"He's not." I pointed to an older, paunchy white man on the TV. He was talking into the camera about an upcoming climate change summit in London. Above his head a globe rotated, but it was a beaming sun of his own face. "He just wants attention. He thinks he's the centre of the universe."

"Well, maybe not him."

"And the reporter is only interested in being famous." The camera switched to a row of politicians, clustering together for a photograph, beaming at the camera. "And that guy is terrified of being invisible, and she is just focused on holding on to everything she's got. He's alright. He's trying, but the rest of them are awful."

He was staring at me. "That's a pretty good summary, actually."

Again, I had that strange feeling that everyone else had been seeing straight and I had been missing it all. "Why is no one doing anything?"

"We need wine." He stood up and went and got a bottle and two glasses. As he sat back down, I watched the people on screen shaking hands.

A new question occurred to me. "If you could prosecute anyone, who would it be?"

"I wouldn't really. That's the point. Everyone is dealing with something. That's why I like your idea so much. It's a lot harder to be annoyed at people for overtaking you too fast or jumping the queue when you can see what they're going through. Why did this person steal, why is he on drugs? What happened to him, not why did he do it."

On the TV a protest march made its way silently across the screen. It switched back to the smug white guy.

He sighed. "Even if they could see it, some people wouldn't care."

"But if they could feel it, maybe that would make all the difference."

The news ended and the credits for the late-night chat show started. More importantly I had a plan.

"Big thoughts tonight," said Callum.

"Yeah," I said.

The TV host strutted out onto the stage. Around his neck a small baby was hanging in a child carrier. It was wailing silently, its face red and blotchy. Its arms were flailing about. But as the lights came up and the applause rang out it stopped crying and clapped its hands and beamed out at the smiling audience, holding its little hands out towards them in supplication.

I took Lobster with me into my room. "I think I know what we are going to do," I said.

Lobster cocked her feelers at me.

"I want to share you." She took a step back. "Just briefly. Just for a few minutes at a time."

She settled down onto the bedside-tabletop like a puppy waiting for instructions.

"I know that you're here to help make the world better and I can't do much about that. But you can. I think we should let other people see what I'm seeing. I think they would be better people for it. If we picked the right ones, they could change everything. Judges, politicians – people with power. What do you think?"

She was watching me, but I couldn't tell what she was thinking.

"Just for a little while. Just until they understand. And then you come back, and we can target the next person. I know, I know; it sounds scary to me too and we're going to have to get close to a whole bunch of important people which isn't going to be easy. But it would be worth it. What do you think?"

She didn't respond and I thought maybe she hadn't heard me. Or maybe she didn't want to do it. I was asking too much of her. She was a little super lobster. Should I just be grateful that she wanted to help me at all and leave it at that?

Then she stood up and turned around. Her legs were doing something complicated, but I couldn't see. When she turned back there was something sitting on the tabletop. It was a little speck, like a grain of sand but dark red. I leaned in and peered at it – it was a little shiny burgundy bubble. Inside there was a tiny black shape.

The shape moved, a little flick. It was an egg.

"What's this for?"

She moved around in a circle and lifted her tail. Underneath there was a whole cluster of eggs, tiny shapes clinging to her stomach.

"They're beautiful," I said.

She turned back to face me and then using her tail she flicked the egg a tiny bit closer to me.

"What's this for?"

She flicked it again.

Then it dawned on me. "For me? For my plan? Seriously?"

I felt a little tearful then. She was right but it was a big sacrifice. All of these people would have lobsters of their own. This was going to change the world. Even better than that, I didn't have to lose her.

Chapter Twenty

The queue was long and winding, which was surprising given the quality of the weather. It was much warmer in London that it had been in Edinburgh when we left but still the wind was chilly. I was nervous. Were any of these people here for anything as mind-bending as I was? They could all have little lobsters, and I would never know. Or they could be genuinely interested in the running of the country, of course.

In front of me was a group of teenage pupils, all talking too loudly with too many gestures. Two of the boys were posturing and preening, the little lion cubs at their feet fighting with sharp teeth and sharper claws. Another group off to one side, joined together by twists of thin, coloured silks, knitting and unknitting almost as fast as the eye could see.

One girl was sitting on the low wall cross-legged reading a book, deliberately ignoring the girl next to her who was jostling her, practically climbing into the lap of a tousle-haired boy. Their heads were together, and they were talking in low voices. If you looked closely you could see their hands merging in and out of each other, in one moment five and then ten fingers entwined. It was sweet.

The girl reading her book had a monkey sitting on her shoulder. It was picking fleas out of her hair and occasionally leaning forward to read from the page. Each time its weight shifted the girl lifted a hand, pushing her blonde hair back from her eyes, and the monkey back into its place. It was clearly heavy. The monkey wasn't happy with the arrangement and shrieked in protest.

The girl was all alone, dealing with something no one else could see. Did the other kids even notice her?

Then I saw another girl further back down the queue. She was also sitting on the wall, looking around her, studiously bored. I noticed that each time she glanced at the blonde-haired girl a little bluebird would appear and swoop around her head. When she looked away again it was gone.

Did the blonde girl know about her admirer? I almost wanted to distract the monkey for a moment, see if I could get her to notice. But that was Cupid's job, not mine. The girl caught my gaze and scowled. I looked away.

Charlotte tapped me on the shoulder.

"Alright, star-gazer. Where did you go?"

"Just people watching."

"Perhaps best not staring at a group of children, though."

"Oh, right."

"They'll be letting us in in a bit. PM's Questions start in about an hour. Have you got the tickets?"

"Yes."

A ripple of activity heralded the arrival of a tall man with steam rising from his shoulders. He came striding up the line muttering something angrily. The kids all started shuffling forwards, protesting or laughing as they picked up their bags.

The bluebird girl was taking longer than the rest. The tall

man, presumably their teacher, gave her a disgusted look but her machinations were working, and she was ready just as the blonde girl walked up to her.

They did a little "after you" dance and smiled at each other. Hooray.

As the line moved forwards, I could hear the teacher, still standing blocking the pavement on the other side of the barrier, mutter, "Oh, for god's sake." As the line moved and we got closer I got a better look at his steaming shoulder. It was a chip, leaking frying oil into his jacket. I couldn't help but smile.

The kids were at the front of the line now, dumping their battered rucksacks on the security table. I looked at Lobster, but she was flying gentle laps around me, taking in all there was to see. I wondered whether she would show up on the X-ray machine and how I'd explain it to Charlotte.

Probably best not to try it, given what happened with Paula.

The kids were finally done and barrelled off into a side room, full of sound and fury. From a distance I could still hear the snarls of the lion cubs.

I plonked my bag down on the melamine table in front of the tall, black-clad security guard. His face had not a trace of humour about it.

"Sharps? Liquids? Laptops?" he said, in the practiced monotone of infinite repetitions.

"Just my phone," I said.

He grunted. His buzz-cut hair and perma-frown made me nervous. What I was doing was probably treason, or insurrection, or something.

Then I noticed his hands. The dark skin was beautifully set off by blobby pink nail polish. As he handed me back my bag I saw there were letters, one per nail, picked out in blue polka dots: D A D D Y.

My grin was involuntary, but it must have been catching because, as he handed me my bag, he smiled, almost in surprise, and wished me a nice day.

Charlotte had been at the desk on the other side of the entrance. As she rejoined me she said, "What's going on with you?"

"What do you mean?"

"Since when did you start charming total strangers?"

"He's wearing his daughter's nail polish to work."

Charlotte glanced over and then leaned in. "No, he's not."

"Metaphorically," I said.

"OK." she gave me another look. "Why are we here? Really? You said this was a girls' trip. I took time off work! And here we are visiting the Houses of Parliament."

"I'm a citizen of this country and I should take an interest."

"Right. Of course." She could not have looked more sceptical. But she followed me up the steps anyway.

Eventually we made it to the visitors' gallery looking down into the debating chamber. We were shown to our benches, one back from the front. The huge space was packed. A riot of gold, green and varnished wood. The noise was incredible.

Charlotte sat down next to me. "So, everything you expected?"

"It's higher than I thought."

"I guess they don't want the hoi polloi popping down and joining in."

"No."

Lobster floated across to the rail, peering over the side. She turned back to look at me. Her claws clicked nervously.

Seeing her poised there on the rail I felt frightened. She

wasn't a tiny little lobsterling anymore. Her paddle of a tail was curled around the clutch of eggs, making flying difficult. The drop down there was huge. What if she got hurt? What if she couldn't make it back? Was the betterment of British politics worth losing Lobster?

I felt my muscles bunch to leap forward and scoop her up and pull her close. But at that moment someone called for quiet with, ironically a lot of noisy banging of something heavy.

The politicians all took a seat and I leaned forward nervously to see what was going to happen. There was a writhing mass of snakes on the floor. I recognised the smug man from the TV – his giant face sun was hard to miss. But it was almost blocked out by all the other spectres filling the room. I ducked as an eagle swooped by. It was like nightmarish Noah's Ark.

At first it seemed like every cliché in the book. But as I watched, in amongst all the animalistic chaos there were other things. A white flag was waving, slowly. Down in the snake pit a single rose was trying to grow. A flock of starlings was circling the rafters, keeping out of the way of the eagle. It was bewildering.

A movement caught my eye and I saw Lobster was already flying forward into the seething mass. Her legs gently sculling she floated serenely downwards. My breath caught.

The flock of starlings raced past and a screech made me jump but the eagle was after the fleeing birds and took no notice of Lobster. A huge bang in the middle of the floor; a cloud of smoke rose up. For some reason everyone was laughing and jeering. Lobster sculled serenely onwards.

Finally, she reached the benches. People were popping to their feet and waving bits of paper but she ignored them all and drifted around to settle above the shoulder of a man lounging on the bench, legs and arms crossed. He looked like the type to have a monocle and was braying with laughter. Lobster dipped down for a second and then launched herself back into the air. From the gallery I couldn't see any more than that, but she seemed happy with what she had done and made her way down the bench to a woman with a red suit, a man who looked like he had just fallen out of bed, and then across the aisle to three more on the other side.

Another flash of gunpowder made me nearly swallow my tongue but finally she was making her way back, paddling through the cloud of smoke. I didn't breathe until she was up to the rail and then, finally, mercifully, back in my hands.

I barely heard or saw anything after that. The noise continued but I was numb. At some point Charlotte touched my arm and I looked into her face. She said something and stood up, so I followed her and let her lead the way. Now she could have all the girls' trip she wanted. Lobster was still nestled in the crook of my crossed arms. I felt shaky and sick.

But as we stepped out of the building the daylight seemed to burst into a note of hope. We had done it. The world was never going to be the same again. I clutched Lobster to me tightly and followed Charlotte back down the street to the Tube.

I was doing my ironing when I saw it.

Callum had the news on, as per usual, and the blond-haired politician came out onto the screen amid a barrage of flashbulbs. At first I thought they were one of the mirages, a testament to his ego, but Callum's eyes went squinty too in the glare.

There were a couple of people standing in front of podia,

looking smug and important. Around them, nestled in amongst the pot plants and porticos were more middle-aged men in suits, holding leather portfolios.

Blondie, or Chancellor of the Exchequer, as he is more commonly known, was looking expectantly at the man on the podium next to him. As the man started to speak I heard thunder. I put the iron on its rest and came around to stand behind Callum on the sofa.

Outside our window the sun shone in a blue sky, so I looked back at the TV to see what mirage was about to appear. The air in front of the man was getting hazy and the thunder was louder. As he continued to talk in a gentle monotone a battalion of cavalry crashed through the door behind him, jostling for room. The horses, wild-eyed and fearsome, were bestridden by muscular men in red uniforms with white plumes billowing from their black helmets. The lead horseman carried an enormous flag that snapped and thrashed in the wind of their arrival.

Then the scene froze. Horses rearing, men high in their saddles, a tableau of might.

The man had stopped talking and turned to the blond politician, clearly giving him his cue to speak. The camera panned out.

The chancellor was just standing there, his face ashen, all bluster gone. He was staring at his colleague like the world had just exploded.

The lead horseman unfroze and turned towards him.

"Get on with it, man," the soldier barked.

The unfortunate recipient opened and closed his mouth like a fish. Then the soldier hefted the giant flag in his hand and threw it for him to catch. Blondie jerked backwards as the huge pole hit him square on the forehead, the crack audible above the twitter of camera shutters. He staggered.

He saw it. He felt it. There was no other explanation. He had a lobster too.

We'd done it!

Callum looked around at me like I was crazy as I whooped around the livingroom. His expression was much the same as the poor chancellor, still standing, astounded, on the TV.

I laughed at them both.

"What's happening?" asked Callum.

"We changed the world!"

"You did?"

"I did!"

Lobster had landed on the TV and was reaching down a long, segmented feeler to stroke a spot on the man's shoulder. She seemed proud.

I whooped again and, leaping over the sofa, hauled Callum to his feet to dance a jig. He resisted at first but then relaxed into it. We span and whirled until we collapsed, panting, on the sofa. We seemed to be all tangled up in something like spider silk, all thin, shiny and sticky. Callum was looking at me like I was crazy, or brilliant, or something. Then he looked away. The news had moved on. There was a report on underfunding in the NHS.

But I was on a roll. "Just you wait," I said. "Just you wait. Everything is about to change."

Chapter Twenty-One

I was on the street, heading towards my cafe. Evan probably already had my sandwich made.

"Laura! Laura!" The woman shouting my name was half the street away. She was running towards me, waving her hand, like someone who was missing their bus.

Behind her the air was hot and crowded with bees. As she ran towards me, they streamed around her head, rising up like a tidal wave, blocking out the sun.

The force of her pushed me back a step. I wanted to turn and run but people were looking.

"Laura Robinson from the TV." It wasn't a question. "You have to help me."

"I'm sorry, I'm on my way somewhere."

"Please. You have to tell me what's wrong with me." As she spoke the bees began landing on her. The whole swarm, tiny body after tiny body, settled on her hair, her skin, her clothes. Soon her whole body was a mass, a formless blob of shifting shapes, merging and flowing like a candle down the back of a radiator.

She was shaking now. No wonder, from my point of view,

but probably baffling from hers. But I couldn't just tell her that her problem was imaginary bees. That would make me sound insane.

"Can you see what my problem is?" repeated the girl.

"I'm sorry. I don't do that anymore." People were starting to stare. I could feel their gazes on me like searchlights.

"Please!"

"What do *you* think the problem is?" Worth a try.

"I don't know. I hurt all over. All day and night. I can't sleep. I feel like I'm going insane. I know you're off duty, or whatever, but I just need someone to listen to me."

"OK. It's OK...?"

"Alba."

"Alba. I want to help you. I do. But I'm not sure what to say. I can see the prickles. They're bees. Hundreds of bees. Everywhere. Crawling all over you."

I waved my hand in the space between us and dislodged a couple of little ones. One landed on the back of my hand. Its feet pinched like needles.

"Ouch." The poor girl was experiencing this all over herself. "I know that sounds crazy but—"

"No. It doesn't," she said. "I mean, it does, but you're the first person who hasn't told me I was imagining it." The girl was crying now. "I've been to so many doctors. They say it's all in my mind. But you can see it, and that means I'm not crazy."

She flung her arms around me. I felt bad. Everything I saw was all in the mind, but I couldn't tell her that. Pain is all in the mind. That doesn't make it any less painful.

"Thank you," she was repeating over and over. The people watching were exchanging looks. I knew those looks.

I patted her cautiously on the back and blew one of the bees off my nose. "That's OK. I do need to go now, though."

"Oh, of course. But do you think you could come with me to my doctor's appointment. Maybe he would listen to you."

I thought about Paula. "He really wouldn't. I'm sorry. I have to go."

"No, I don't mean now. It's not until next week. I'll pay you. I'll do anything."

"I'm sorry. It really won't help. Trust me."

"But what am I supposed to do? No one will listen to me."

"I'm sorry."

She didn't follow me, just stayed standing on the pavement. She looked like a pillar of black, wriggling salt when I looked back.

Lunch was no fun after that. Even in my corner table, even with Evan asking about my day, all I could see was that girl and her life companions.

How awful to live like that. And I was doing what, exactly? Trying to change the world by making the rich and powerful see more clearly. Like Mother Teresa, or Gandhi. How was that helping this girl, or any of these people whose lives were horrible, one day after another?

Lobster seemed to sense my mood. She came out and sat on the table.

I looked around. Evan's brain cloud was smaller today. At another table, a man seemed to be holding himself at gunpoint. A woman passing the window on the street was walking through falling snow.

What good was I if I could see all this but I couldn't help them?

I put my headphones in and pretended to dial. "I have to talk to you," I said to Lobster. "I'm going to do something about all this. We need to do something more."

Lobster clacked her pincers together and shuffled her feet. She seemed pleased so I took that as assent.

I went to see Carol at the Community Centre with my next idea. Surprisingly, she was instantly on board. Her face lit up when I explained what I wanted to do. Within half an hour I had a date, a room booking and a small budget for refreshments.

I walked back to the lounge feeling slightly befuddled. This was turning into a Thing.

Lillian was waiting for me, the only other resident apart from the ubiquitous Helen.

She looked pleased when I hurried in.

"Well, what a difference a fortnight makes," she said, beaming.

"Yeah," I said, stopping myself from looking at Lobster who was hovering off my left shoulder. "I'm feeling much better."

"How did it go with Carol? Is she in?"

"Yes. She's excited about helping the residents who don't get much in the way of visitors." We both didn't look over at Helen.

"I've pulled together a box of my sheep. It's in my room. I tried to find the neatest ones but they're a bit shabby at best."

"They'll be perfect. I just need to get people's attention."

"Did you come up with a name yet?" asked Lillian.

"Hey Ewe."

"Hey me?"

"No, e-w-e."

Lillian chuckled. "I like it."

I glanced across at Helen, sitting as ever on the other side of the room staring out of the window. Lillian turned to see what I was looking at.

"It's great what you're doing but it still might not be the kind of thing that will make her happy."

I could taste the dust from here. "Not happy. I don't even care if she has fun. I just want her to feel a little less lonely, just a tiny bit."

"Well, regardless, I think it's a lovely idea, and it would be a relief to be rid of all those sheep. Sometimes I think they might bury me alive."

That afternoon I went out onto the High Street with a couple of the little sheep in hand. The first shop I went into was the gift shop on the corner. It had a jaunty awning and seemed friendly. I pushed open the door.

A small step forward and I found I had entered a chrome and white emporium. An exalted palace of Rolex watches, zirconium earrings and Radley handbags. Halogen lights bounced off glass display cases into bright shards, making my eyes water.

A woman looked up from behind the polished aluminium counter. Her gaze was sharp.

"Can I help at all? Looking for something special?"

I looked around at the expensive pens and watches. Our little dowel sheep felt shoddy in comparison. I hesitated. This was a stupid idea. No one wanted little handmade sheep from the local community centre.

Lobster settled herself gently on my shoulder and as she did a rabbit lolloped out from behind the counter. It was sporting a moustache and had a waistcoat on. It sat back on its hind legs and waved at me.

The woman's gaze was like ice, but the little rabbit gave me courage.

"I'm here from the community centre up on Orchard Street. We're holding an event in a month's time and I was wondering if you would be interested in helping."

"Are you looking for donations?" she asked coldly. But, even so, the rabbit shuffled a little closer.

"No, we're wondering if we could put these out in your shop."

I put one of the little sheep down on her shiny counter. The label flopped open and an inexpertly written *Hey Ewe* was front and centre.

The woman stared at it for a moment. I thought she was maybe recoiling in horror but then saw her eyes flickering. She was reading it.

The rabbit suddenly leapt onto the counter making me jump. It sniffed the little wooly thing then looked at me and back at the woman. Then it did a cartwheel.

"I don't understand," said the woman. Her face was pinched and closed. "Do you want me to sell these?"

"No, just to have a few in the shop. It's for an event we're holding at the community centre – like a celebration. People can take them for free. If they want to, they can come along on the day for tea and cake. And they can have their sheep presented to someone that they've brought with them, for a small donation. Like an awards ceremony."

"But what if they just take them and don't come back?"

"That's OK. We've got loads and not everyone will want to come. Maybe they'll give them to a friend – and we've achieved the same thing just in private."

The little rabbit started nibbling the edge of the label. The woman showed no sign of interest at all, but the rabbit spoke otherwise.

I plunged on. "It might get some people's attention and even if ten show up that would be wonderful. It would be great for the residents – we're hoping some people might bring one along for them."

She picked up the little sheep and examined it. She probably thought we were crazy giving them away. Then she suddenly smiled.

"I'm happy to help," she said. "I can put a box on the counter."

I stumbled over my tongue in gratitude. "That would be great."

She picked up the sheep and turned it over. "How many do you have?"

I thought about Lillian's room, every surface fluffy with sheep. "Hundreds. More than we know what to do with."

"These labels are going to take you forever to write. Can I offer an alternative? I have some great software and some nice card stock." She indicated the beautifully crafted signs attached to each of the gleaming shelves. "I could make the labels for you." The rabbit was hopping up and down.

"Really? If you're sure."

"I'd like to. My mum used that community centre before she died. It's a lovely place. I'd like to help."

"Thank you so much."

As I left her shop three sheep lighter, with her business card stuffed in my pocket, I thought about Laura from four months ago before Lobster. She would never have done that. She hadn't known what she was missing.

Chapter Twenty-Two

Unfortunately, I still had to go into work. There was only so long I could call in sick. There was a chance that walking out on Patrick would have no repercussions. Rachel had said it didn't matter either way whether I dated him, that the contract was secure. It was probably going to be fine.

I dressed with a bit more care anyway, picking one of Sandy's outfits exactly as she would have worn it. If we'd still been speaking she would have been able to give me great advice on how to style it out, convince them it was just a little nothing. How to dazzle them, her speciality.

The tram ride was a little too short for my liking. Why is that always the way? A journey that normally takes hours and is filled with noise and spectacle seemed to take only minutes. Clearly no one else going in to work today at all.

Rashda was all smiles when I came in. So far so good. We talked about what she watched on TV, the crazy plot twist in *EastEnders*. Scripts are useful things.

The open plan office was bustling as normal when I walked through the double doors. No one looked up, pointed, or laughed. Not even their spectres paid any attention. OK then.

My emails were similarly inoffensive. Maybe Patrick was just going to let it go.

My phone rang. It was Reception "Hi, Laura. Tom asked if you can go up to his office for a sec."

Maybe not.

Rachel and Tom were both in there. Tom behind the desk in full regalia, his plumes waving regally in the breeze. Rachel didn't meet my eye.

Tom indicated the chair that had been pulled up in front of his desk. It was a hard wooden one. In the corner I could see the other, plush, leather chair, had been shoved out to make way. Oh, for god's sake.

I sat down respectfully. There was still a chance this was a simple dressing down. Yes, sir. No, sir. I've learned my lesson, sir.

Tom had his hands clasped in front of him and pressed his lips up against the steeple of his index fingers. I could almost hear his expression: *oh dear, oh dear, oh dear.*

"Laura, you're probably wondering why I called you in here today," he said.

"I'm going to guess it has something to do with Patrick," I said.

He looked surprised. Was he expecting me to grovel?

He leaned ever closer. "Laura, Patrick is our best client and a personal friend. I'm wondering whether you can explain to me what happened."

I looked at Rachel, but she was just watching me sadly.

"Tom, I'm sorry if he is upset but he's just not who I thought he was."

He sat back with a sigh and looked up at Rachel. She shook her head and shrugged. Then she turned back to me with a

175

strange expression. "He says you stood him up."

"Um, no. I, just... left."

"He also says that he was coerced into signing the contract without legal representation present and therefore the contract is void."

"What?"

"But that's not true. Rachel, tell him."

Tom raised his hand and Rachel stepped back, looking like a spanked puppy.

Tom glared at me though his visor. "As a long-term client and friend, I'm minded to let him cancel the sale."

"What about Rachel's bonus?"

Both Rachel and Tom looked surprised.

"What about it?" asked Tom. "Contract's void. So's the bonus. She's lucky I don't fire her."

Rachel cowered back.

"No, this is bollocks," I said, suddenly on my feet. "Patrick is getting back at me because I dumped him. This has nothing to do with Rachel at all. Or the contract. He's lying."

"Laura!"

"Well, he is. Call him out on it."

Tom stood up so we were squared off across the desk. He was a lot taller than me. I heard a clank of spurs. "Patrick is a valuable client with a reputation for professionalism. You have been here five minutes. I don't think I'm going to take your word over his."

Sitting in that chair I had the strange sensation of being about five years old.

"But I'm telling the truth! Rachel?"

Tom stood up. "I think we're done here. You can pack up your things. You're fired, obviously."

176

I felt my mouth open and close, like a fish. There were no words. There had to be words. I just couldn't find them. I watched the two of them walk out of the room, utterly unable to do anything to stop it.

Just like that, I was unemployed.

I had thought… what had I thought? That they would believe me? That they would be sympathetic? Or at least that Rachel would back me up.

I walked out into the street with my head spinning. My heels felt too tall and clunky, the fancy clothes chafed. I didn't even want this anyway. If that's the kind of people they were I was better off without them. I turned towards my cafe.

Two coffees in and I had already put the whole sorry ordeal behind me. I had more important things to do anyway. And there, at least, I was actually making a difference.

"What's that?"

I looked up at Evan as he put another cup of coffee down in front of me. He was looking at my notebook. I moved my writing hand instinctively, so it covered the words.

"Ideas," I said.

"Anything good?"

What to say to that? Just planning on taking over the world with a fecund lobster and her offspring. But then we were kind of friends now and it's not like he would know what I was talking about. "Ways to change the world."

"Just a small thing, then." He was smiling now.

"Just a small one."

"How's that working out for you?"

"Pretty good so far. I think I've taken care of the politicians. Most of them, anyway."

177

He looked a bit surprised at that. "You have?"

"Hopefully. They seem to be responding well. I'm working out who to target next."

"After the politicians," he said slowly.

"Yes."

He opened his mouth and then closed it again. "To target."

"Yes." I sipped my coffee. It was good, as ever.

Lobster tapped her claws sharply on the table. She was looking at Evan.

What?

He was still standing there, now he was looking horrified. I ran back over my words in my mind. Ah.

"TV show," I said, and waved the notebook at him. "Guests for my TV show."

"Oh!" It was a bit too loud and a bit too long – he was relieved. I suppressed the urge to snigger.

As he wandered back over to the counter Lobster gave me a glare.

Well, what was I supposed to say? I looked down at the list of industry leaders, judges, and media moguls. I could hardly say it was a list of my crushes or anything, given who was on there.

Besides, what I was doing was kind of dodgy. I was getting access to the most powerful people I could think of and trying to make them change their entire view of the world. It was a sort of plot.

My phone pinged. Dad again. Still trying to get me to meet for dinner.

I felt a twinge of annoyance and guilt. This visit was really bad timing. He had come all the way from Australia to basically sit in a hotel and wait for his daughter to agree to see him. But

I was right in the middle of something important and dealing with him was the last thing I needed.

I went back to my planning. Callum could probably get me into some kind of judicial setting but the industry and media people were harder. I needed an access point, like an event or a meeting. But how could I get invited to either? For the first time I cursed my small life with its lack of red carpet invitations.

As the week went on I kept myself busy with the plans for the event. But I had one eye on the TV, waiting to see what we had done. It was a week where I had dreamed of every possible outcome. Perhaps a new aid package for low-paid workers, a ban on all plastic packaging, perhaps world peace.

On the Thursday they announced another press conference for that evening. A different room this time; more of a community centre than a grand, palatial hotel. Good sign.

I sat glued to the TV, waiting for the world to change.

The chancellor walked out into the crowd of photographers. His trademark swagger was gone, replaced by a smaller, more contained walk.

To my surprise a small, sharp-faced woman walked out and took up position next to him. I had seen her in pictures online during my week of research and scenario planning. His estranged wife who had moved out last year after the fifth sex scandal.

The noise in the room dropped off as he stood there silently, head bowed.

What was he going to say? A new budget? Fairer taxes? An end to corporate loopholes?

Callum was sitting on the sofa, feet up on the footstool, one toe tapping. Did he know something was coming too?

The announcer on the TV had run out of space-filling and the silence billowed out from the tableau. The sharp-faced wife stepped forward and took one of his tightly clenched hands in hers. He looked across at her and both of their faces relaxed into a private smile. The smile transformed them both.

"I'm here to make an announcement," he said, turning to the cameras but still holding tight to her hand. "As of this morning I let the prime minister know that I am retiring from politics."

"No!"

Callum looked over at my shriek and raised an eyebrow. He put both feet on the floor with an audible thump and turned back to the TV, his elbows on his knees.

"After a lot of soul searching, I've made the decision that I'm leaving so that I can spend more time with my family. I understand now what matters and it's time for them to come first." His wife smiled to herself.

By the end of the news I was almost in tears. What a waste!

Callum was watching me. "I thought you said he was an arse," he said.

"He was," I said. "But he was about not to be. Dammit. Never mind. There were two more."

"Two more what?" He was looking puzzled.

"Two more possibilities. The foreign secretary and the weaselly advisor chap. And some people on the other side too."

"What are you talking about?"

Lobster was fast asleep on my lap. I rested a hand on her armoured skin. "Not to worry, this will still work."

Chapter Twenty-Three

Thankfully, I had too many other things to do to dwell. Callum caught me coming out of my bedroom on the way to the TV studios.

"Off out again? I feel like I haven't seen you all week."

"Yeah. Off to watch the taping of the *News Quiz*."

"Really?"

"Yeah, they've got a senior politician hosting it this time. And the guy who owns all those newspapers. It's perfect."

"Perfect?"

"Two for one."

Not that he knew what I was on about.

"Isn't that the fourth taping you've been to?"

"Yup, and three live debates. We're making progress. Oh, and I forgot to tell you, one of your senior judges was there at the last debate. Just you wait – your legal problems will soon be over."

"Huh?"

"You'll see." I edged towards the door. Didn't want to be sat near the back and make poor Lobster have to fly even further.

"Will I see you later?"

"Hmm, filming finishes at midnight and then I'm in the community centre all tomorrow. Maybe Sunday? No, that's the red carpet thing. I don't know. I'll see you soon, though."

"Laura?"

"Yes."

He looked like he was about to put a hand on my shoulder which irritated me. I kept backing away towards the front door.

"Are you OK?" he asked.

"I'm fine," I said, putting on my coat. He couldn't possibly understand what I was achieving. But he'd see. "I'm fixing things. What could be better than that? Bye."

A caught a glimpse of his face as I closed the door. He looked unhappy.

Chapter Twenty-Four

When I opened the door to the back room of the community centre, I found a huge pile of donations and sheep waiting for me. We were one week away from the Fun Day. It was coming along nicely but there was still so much to do.

The room was almost too full to get into. The pile of sorted goods in the corner was heartening but the other half still needed doing. Lillian's sheep were perched on top of the giant pile, making it impossible to sort until I attended to them first. The new ones were obvious from the lack of pretty cardboard labels around their necks. They were breeding. Every day there were more of them.

I picked up the nearest one and put it, experimentally, on the table. It wobbled. About a third of them had wonky legs. I picked up the sanding pad and started the long slow task of creating better balance.

It was lucky that I had been fired really. Because helping people was turning out to be a full-time job. I had assumed the point of super-Lobster was to make all of this easier, but she only really excelled at identifying the problems I had to fix.

The night before had been a bad one. I had rearranged my pillow far too many times for it to have been a good sleep. But that wasn't important.

Lobster hovered near the door, up high – out of the sawdust cloud, I supposed. Lucky her. Her feelers were twitching to and fro.

By the time I left there were four more stable sheep. The afternoon was gone, my throat was raw and my eyes were streaming. But it was fine.

The stairs to the flat felt mountainous. My ankles hurt. Even Lobster seemed tired after all our hard work.

Callum was standing in the hall when I opened the door.

"Hi," I said.

He looked uncomfortable for some reason. "Hi," he said.

"I'm off for a shower," I said.

"Right. OK," he said.

I turned to go to my room but he called my name. Behind him, standing in the middle of the living-room, was Charlotte. She was holding her hands clasped in front of her like a Primary School Head Teacher.

"Can we have a word?" asked Callum.

This did not bode well. I followed him in.

"Coffee?" asked Charlotte. Her voice was weirdly high pitched.

"No." I sat on the arm of the armchair. "Guys, you're freaking me out. I'm tired and dusty. What's going on?"

"We're worried about you," said Callum, quietly, from over by the kitchen counter

"Why?"

Charlotte perched on the sofa and beckoned me over. Lobster floated towards her so I went. "You're doing too much."

I sighed. Always doing too much or doing too little. Too ambitious or not ambitious enough.

"I'm helping people. What's wrong with that?"

"Nothing," she said, clasping my hand in hers. "I just think you need to slow down a bit."

"You've barely slept since your dad got here," said Callum.

I pulled my hand back from Charlotte and glared at him. "What's Dad got to do with anything?"

He came over to the table with a plate of pastries and a glass of water. Pastries again? What was he trying to pull?

"You're avoiding him."

"Of course I am! But that's what call blocking on my phone is for. That's not why I'm busy. I'm busy because there's a job to do."

Callum pushed the pastries and the water closer. Patronising arse.

"What job?" he said.

"Oh yes, very clever. Just because I'm unemployed. I think you'll find there's more to the world than paid employment," I snapped.

He didn't answer that one. Just shook his head, looking pained. Hah!

"I'm running the Community Centre Fun Day if you must know. Amongst other things. Important things." Lobster crept a little closer, her claws reaching out towards me.

Charlotte took a pastry but didn't take a bite. "I'm just worried you're overdoing it."

I glared at them. How dare they talk down to me like this.

"I cannot bloody win with you people. I'm too passive, now I'm too busy. I don't talk to enough people, I don't do enough with my life. Now I'm doing too much? Pick one!"

Callum didn't seem affected by my outburst. He leaned forward and said, "I'm not your mum, Laura. Charlotte's not Sandy. There was nothing wrong with you before."

I tried to retort but there was suddenly a lump in my throat. Lobster was staring at me hard. She raised one claw and pointed at Callum. *Et tu, Lobster?*

"But I'm doing what you told me to," I said to her. "I'm helping."

She leapt lightly into the air and floated close to my cheek. I felt the air from her tail fan like a caress.

I had a sudden image of brushing her away from my face. When had I done that? In the back room, this afternoon. And before that in the cafe. And before that—

What was I doing?

"… alone," Callum was saying.

"What?"

"I said, you don't have to do any of this alone."

Lobster drifted back into view. She looked sad.

"But I do, though."

"Why?" said Charlotte.

"Because I'm the only one who can."

Lobster. My Lobster. Selflessly giving up her children to change the world. What had I done that was even close to matching that sacrifice? I had to make it up to her.

Charlotte's hand appeared on my hand. "Maybe just take a break. A little one."

Her hand on mine looked like a dead fish. I couldn't tell, resting on my knee, where my hand began and her hand ended. Was that my knee feeling the pressure of her hand, or my hand, or was it my hand interpreting the resistance of my knee? It all felt the same.

Lobster came and settled next to our hands. She was bigger than our hands put together. When had she got so big? She laid her claw gently on top, like we were team-mates doing a cheer. I felt something inside me give a little.

Callum walked back to the counter. His laptop was sitting open and he spun it around. I studied his face, lit up blue from the screen, wishing, not for the first time, that Lobster would tell me a little something about what was going on inside that head of his.

"So," he said. "I found us a canal boat for the weekend."

"Sorry?"

"A canal boat. Just a little one. Just for the weekend so you're not away too long."

I stared at him.

"Only if you want to. Just an idea."

He pushed the laptop across the counter so I went to look. A canal boat nestled in green countryside, overlooking some immaculate valley. The people on the boat were laughing, their arms around each other. I felt the muscles in my shoulders involuntarily relax.

I looked back at Lobster and Charlotte on the sofa. They both nodded.

Maybe I did need a break. A few days away from that back room. Just a short one. While the dust settled. By then Lobster's eggs would surely have hatched and the world would be a different place.

"OK, I'll take a break."

Chapter Twenty-Five

We picked up the boat near Oxford and almost immediately were out in the countryside. Callum had given me the tiller straight off, claiming a chronic confusion between left and right. He went off to unpack and explore. I found myself sitting alone on the back of a great iron monstrosity, staring down into the murky water of the canal, watching the stinging nettles pass by picturesquely. The boat was huge and unwieldy, and the throbbing of the engine travelled up my legs and rattled my teeth. We were being overtaken by elderly walkers out with their dogs. Passing cyclists seemed to flash by in a blur.

It should have been irritating, aggravating. Instead, as I got used to the weight of the tiller and the glacial speed that the boat turned, I started noticing things. The tangle of branches on the bank. A tiny hole between the knotted roots – maybe a water vole burrow. A flash of blue revealed itself as a kingfisher sitting, almost invisible, on a branch whose twigs were trailing little v-shaped ripples in the water.

In the absence of any talking to do my mind became trans-fixed by the tall reeds lining long stretches of the riverbank, a kind of visual white noise. Endless strands rippling and flowing in the breeze. Something about them reached inside my head and turned the speedo down to idle.

A cup of tea appeared on the roof in front of me, the steam barely blown backwards by the achingly slow movement of the boat. Callum popped his head out from the cabin.

"Just what I needed, thank you," I said.

He put a packet of biscuits down next to the tea and came up on deck to join me.

"This is lovely," I said above the throbbing of the engine. "The view is amazing. We're lucky with the weather."

Callum took a sip from his tea, looking out at the bank. "I've a proposal. No pleasantries allowed. Say something big, or nothing at all."

I frowned at him but he just handed me my teacup from the roof.

I opened my mouth to say cheers but that probably counted as a pleasantry. What on earth were we going to talk about?

Nothing, it turned out.

We chugged on through the countryside, over an aqueduct which gave us the perfect vista over fields as far as the eye could see. An aeroplane went past, at what looked like eye height. But apparently, I wasn't allowed to comment on any of it at all.

Two hours we had been going and we had gone seven miles. We turned another corner, and a row of large houses hove into view. Each of them with an acre of lawn and weeping willow trees on the bank. One had a carefully manicured pier. It was covered in metalwork flamingos. I nodded towards it. Callum inclined his head in supplication. Not even metal flamingos could tempt him then.

I drank my tea, and another cup appeared a while later. I ate another biscuit.

"What happened with your dad?" asked Callum, suddenly.

I glanced across at him, but he was just staring at a passing tumbledown barn.

"Nothing. Everything. It's a big old mess. I tried to apologise but then I still don't understand why he left. I'm still angry with him for leaving."

"What do you have to apologise for?"

I looked at him. Normally people made polite noises and said things like "families are hard", "two sides to every story", "bastard, narcissist, deadbeat dads." That last one was Charlotte, obviously.

The boat gently but firmly pushed a path through the weedy water. The ripples edged up to the bank, as if worried about causing offence. If you slowed the engine far enough, just as the instructional video had suggested, the wake wouldn't reach the banks at all; lost in the directionless water.

"When I was little, I told everyone that my childminder was bullying me."

"Were they?"

"Mrs Poole, she…" The woman's toothy smile loomed in my mind's eye. The tiny basement flat with the neat-as-a-pin back garden filled with colourful plastic toys. "She was a great favourite of Sandy's. Sandy loved it there."

"And you?"

"I didn't take to her as well. But that's normal, I guess. Different kids. Different personalities. I was always a lot more sensitive than Sandy, Mum said.

"There were loads of kids at first, and another woman working with her. Then people kept leaving until it was just her and me." And then the coloured plastic toys had gone too. Didn't matter really, the garden was off limits by then. "It

190

wasn't fun anymore."

"Why did your parents make you stay?"

"She was a friend of my mum's and she got divorced and had no money, so we had to support her." As I spoke, I could almost hear the gnome's voice, coaching me in my head. "She was a nice woman from a good family who had fallen on hard times."

The words stuck on my tongue and prevented me from saying any more. Pleasantries, that's what I needed now. Lots and lots of lovely neutral camouflaging words.

Callum quietly waited for me to say more.

"I was lonely, so I made up an imaginary friend. Her name was Evelyn." The name stuck in my throat, but I said it anyway. "She was always getting into trouble and causing drama. Mrs Poole put her 'in the coal hole'." I did air quotes. "To keep her out of the way. I told Mum and Dad I didn't want to go there anymore but they said I was being silly."

A barky dog ran by. Its owner raised his hand to us in a friendly salute. We raised ours back.

"Go on," said Callum when the walker had gone past.

My voice was small when it came out. "So I told them it had happened to me."

"OK."

"My dad believed me. He and Mum got into these huge fights about it." Little flashes of memories swirled in the water. The shouting and breaking glass. The police interview where I was too scared to speak. Mrs Poole's pinched face in my living room. Mum apologising over and over. "In the end my mum got it out of me that it had all been a lie. Dad kept pushing it. It became about how he was trying to save me, like some superhero complex. Even after they got divorced, he wouldn't leave it alone. Then one day he just left. Went to live in Australia. Sandy and Mum haven't spoken to him since."

"How old were you?"

"Five." Such destruction and I had only been five.

"That's awful," he said.

I looked away to the bank so he couldn't see the tears in my eyes.

"I'm so sorry that happened to you," he said.

I looked at him in surprise. "To me?"

"You hated the place so much that you had to make something up to get out of there. It must have been awful there."

"I... I've never really thought about it."

"Whatever happened after that is not your fault. You were five. Your parents could have handled it in about fifty different ways. If they broke up over it that's not down to you."

I opened my mouth to retort but the only things in my head all sounded suspiciously gnome-like. Surely there was something else I could say.

Callum beat me to it.

"More tea?"

"Um, OK, thanks."

When he brought the tea up he didn't reopen our conversation and I didn't either. I had so many thoughts swirling around in my head.

By dusk we had travelled just fifteen miles. We could probably still get a Chinese delivered. But Callum had been busy, and supper was already bubbling on the little stove. I nudged the boat in towards the bank and in the half light we tied it to the arm-co. When I killed the engine, the silence flowed in like a wave. I felt myself rocking back from its relentless pressure.

We were stopped next to a field of cows. As the initial wave passed, I started to hear the rustle of their feet, the snorts of pleasure as they pulled at the grass. A bird swooped down, perilously close to the canal surface, a tiny aeronaut performing acrobatics for her supper.

The diesel fumes cleared, replaced by the smell of bolognese. My stomach growled. The biscuits had been a long time ago.

I felt dazed, disconnected. But also hungry, and hungry I could deal with.

The cabin was snug, the cooking heat still hung in the air. Callum was pouring wine into two comically small wine glasses. The table was set with placemats showing jaunty-hatted canal boat captains and jolly painted barges.

I squeezed into the padded bench behind the table. I scattered cheese over my spaghetti and took a bite; it was delicious, but I wasn't supposed to say so. This was such a stupid rule.

"I got called in for a disciplinary yesterday," Callum said into the silence.

My hand stilled halfway to my mouth. I thought of the range of possible responses, editing them for pleasantness. "Why?"

"I was inspired by you," he smiled.

"Me?" What had I done?

He was sitting on the little stool. He hadn't eaten anything yet, was just sipping wine.

He took another sip of wine. A gulp really. "My job sucks. But being a lawyer does suck. That's why you make a lot of money. You squirrel it away and then retire at fifty to the countryside somewhere and paint."

"You paint?"

"No." He laughed. "But every time I talk to you about

193

changing the world a little piece of me wants to take the house in the countryside and all the terrible paintings I might one day do and burn them to the ground."

"What are you going to do?"

"Quit, I think. Do something else. New horizons."

New horizons? Something squirmed in my chest. He was leaving? It was my turn to take a gulp of wine. It burned in my throat. "I don't think you should quit because of something I've said to you."

"Why not? All the things you've done this year. I think you're really brave."

"I'm not brave. I wish I could go back to who I was before."

"Before?"

"Before this year, before the new job, before Paula, before seeing my dad, before…" *Lobster.*

He went quiet then.

The spag bol was getting cold but I found I couldn't eat it. The wine, however, was nearly gone.

"I think you should be proud," he said into his wine. "Leaving an unhealthy relationship. Setting up on your own. You've achieved a lot. Sometimes it's better to be single than to be with someone who could be the wrong person."

What to say to that? He was looking at me intently. I had a few choice phrases I could trot out but there was a rule now. I had nothing big to say so I said nothing at all.

So much change. And just when you thought all the changes were done, something else happened. Someone else went away. I stood up abruptly. "I'm going to bed."

I lay in my bunk, feeling the boat rock slightly as Callum moved about the main cabin. I heard the water pump go and the splash of him doing the dishes. That's what you get for banning pleasantries. It didn't matter anyway. He was going to go off and find new horizons, so he'd be gone soon.

This is why you don't let people in.

After a while, the sounds quietened. I heard the hatch slide closed and the rocking as he stepped onto shore to walk along the path to his front hatch. It rocked again as he climbed back on. It went quiet and the lights went out.

The boat was in darkness. The sounds of the nighttime soaked through the thin metal hull. The sick feeling in my stomach wasn't shifting. The flimsy curtains at the windows did nothing to block out the moonlight so I twitched them aside.

I thought back to what Callum had said. That I was taking too much responsibility for what had happened. I lay on the narrow bunk staring up at the ghostly clouds and tried to remember, something I usually tried to avoid. But no matter what I just couldn't remember what it was like at Mrs Poole's, just what I had been told. I couldn't shake the feeling that there was something missing from the story. I caught snatches of half-remembered conversations.

A little bit of difficulty never hurt anybody.
I'm scared.
You're too old to be afraid of the dark.
Please, Mummy
Stop making such a fuss.
Help me.
I don't believe you.
Let me out.

Where was this coming from? Even lying in direct moonlight the boat felt like it was getting darker. The walls were closing in and I couldn't breathe. I tasted coal dust.

Then I was climbing up out of my bed, slipping my feet into my loafers and pulling my coat on. I hurried up to the back of the boat. Callum had left the saloon spotless, of course. Everything in its place.

I sat on the padded bench and poured a large glass of wine. What had happened?

I took another deep breath and another large gulp of wine. This boat was a nice place. Just because it was dark didn't mean it was dangerous.

As I stared out of the window into the shrouded darkness a flash of light caught my eye. It was gone in a second. Had I imagined it?

No, there it was. A shooting star.

I carefully opened the back hatch so as not to make any noise and slipped out onto the deck. The boat rocked gently in its cradle but nothing changed. I perched on the rail and stared up into the sky.

Another star fell. Beautiful.

Another one.

I got my phone out and looked to see if there was anything expected that night. The news was full of the Pleiades meteor shower. I looked at my watch. 1am. It was due to peak at 2am. If I couldn't sleep, I could at least watch the display.

My breath huffed in the cold air. I slipped back down below. Fetching a sofa cushion and my duvet, I made a nest on the light curve of the roof, snug between the boat hook and the life buoy.

So much of my life had been like this. Sitting in the dark, watching the show. A silent, polite figure, not bothering anyone. It was the best way to observe the world. I was an

196

expert at it.

For over two hours flashes of brilliant limelight streaked across the sky. The icy white streaks, obscured by the clouds of my breath, obscured by a curious blurring.

My cheeks felt cold and when I reached up my hands came away wet.

The birds woke me, in my bed, in the morning. That and the smell of bacon. The narrow bed groaned as I shifted my weight. I was still wearing my coat so I padded through into the kitchen.

Callum was turning rashers on the little grill. He pointed to a pot of coffee on the table. It smelled heavenly.

I sipped from mine.

"Sleep well?" It was automatic. I couldn't help it.

Callum smiled ruefully and ignored what I'd said. No pleasantries. But what do you say when you bear your soul to someone that you like and then they announce that they're leaving?

"Do you want to talk about what we said yesterday?" he asked, moving the bacon from the grill onto slices of white bread.

"Um, no."

"OK."

He brought the plate over to the table.

"Are you going to go and see your dad again?" asked Callum.

"Yes. I think I have to."

"That's good." He upended most of the ketchup bottle onto his sandwich. I was going to miss him.

"I'm going to get the engine started," I said.

He nodded.

I picked up a rasher of bacon and took it up on deck with me. It steamed in the cold morning air. The cows were back in the field again, blowing clouds.

I turned the key and the engine exploded into life. No more space for deep conversations. Through the hatch I could see Callum, still sitting at the table.

Chapter Twenty-Six

Dad was waiting in the hotel lobby. He looked like he belonged in the marble-floored, beige-walled opulence in his suede jacket and open collared shirt. I tried not to mind the looks I was getting in my canal boat jeans and fleece.

He smiled when he saw me. I raised a hand. Then we both did that awkward walk towards each other thing where you have to avoid staring straight into each other's eyes as your smile fades to a rictus, but the only other option is to look rudely away and pretend you are interested in the crown mouldings, or that woman's shirt over there.

Finally, we met in front of the desk. He stepped forward and kissed me on the cheek and we both chuckled a bit at how awkward it was. So far, so scripted.

"How are you?" he asked, predictably.

"Fine thanks, how are you?"

"Do you want a coffee here, or...?"

"No. Do you mind if we go somewhere else?" *Somewhere less intimidating.*

"Of course. Where do you have in mind?"

The cafe felt like balm after too many long streets of small talk and pleasantries. Evan raised a hand from behind the counter – we had come so far – and I raised one back. The window table was free of giant elephants – at least other people's – so we took it.

I left Dad looking way too overdressed and went up to the counter.

"Usual?" asked Evan.

At that moment I could have climbed over the counter and hugged him. Instead, I nodded.

"And for your... client? Interviewer?"

"My...?" Lobster and I looked at each other. I felt a hysterical bubble of laughter rise up. Lobster caught it and did a backflip instead.

Evan a was looking at me, grinning. "No?"

"No. That's my dad."

"Ah, sorry. What'll he have?"

"I have no idea. Same as me?"

He nodded and put his book under the counter. I wanted to go with it. Curl up under the counter and hand him up his notebook when his inspiration struck. Better than going back to the table.

"I'll bring it over."

"Thanks."

"You're welcome."

No more avoiding the conversation. I walked back to the table. But this was better than the alternative. Lobster would help. Maybe I could finally bring this stupid visit to an end.

I slid into the seat opposite him. Lobster came and settled on my shoulder. We eyed him beadily.

"I'm really glad we're doing this," he said.

Pleasantries.

"I'm angry with you for leaving," I said.

He looked alarmed. "That's fair enough."

"You can't change everything by taking me out for coffee."

"Also fair." Still so calm. Didn't he feel like the worst person in the whole entire world?

"But I also need to understand why you just left. After we all… found out the truth." His mouth pursed slightly. "Why did you just leave?"

Evan appeared at the table with the coffees and two plates of brownies balanced on his forearms. "Anything else you need, just ask," he said to me. I smiled at him, as much as I could muster. He gave my dad a hard look as he left, and I was able to let go of my grip on the table a bit.

Dad took a sip of his coffee and grimaced. I saw him glance at the sugar on the next table. I fixed him in place with my glare.

He sighed. "I was exhausted." As he spoke the suitcase appeared near his feet. The zip slowly started to open itself. "The lawyers, the courtrooms, the visitation centre. I felt broken."

The words dribbled out of the case and onto the floor, like puddles of urine.

"What courtrooms?"

He looked at me, puzzled. "The whole custody battle."

"What custody battle? You tried to get custody?"

He looked me right in the eye then. "You didn't know that?"

"No!"

His eyes closed and his head sunk into his hands. "I knew it," his voice was muffled. "I knew she lied to you."

I had a sudden flashback to Sandy, as a small girl, singing at me while I cried: *cowardly, cowardly custard*, except she wasn't

201

singing *custard* she was singing *custody.* And Mum shouting those words at my dad, "…never get custody. Over my dead body."

The room swam for a second, lightly blurring and shifting. When it refocused, the world looked different. I shook my head, allowing all the clicky little tiles to fall into place.

"Did she give you my letters?"

I shook my head. Not being allowed to fetch the post on my birthday, Mum insisting on doing the privacy settings on all of my mobile phones.

"But why? Why didn't she want me to talk to you?"

"I think she was afraid of what I would say."

"What would you have said?"

"First of all, that I tried. I tried to be there for you. I failed, and I'm sorry, and that I want to be in your life, even after I let you down like that."

"Then why go to Australia?"

He sighed again. "It was torture, living here. Being so close to you girls but unable to see you, hug you. And then I met Pam. And she was kind and loving. And her children liked me. And when it was time for her to move back to Australia, she asked me to go. And I did. I thought it would ease the pain."

"Did it?" I wasn't sure I even wanted to know.

He shook his head and I felt instantly relieved. "But I did make a life. I had met Pam. I was lucky." He shrugged at my scowl. But what was he supposed to say – sorry?

"Sorry," he said.

He wanted me. He wanted us.

My brain pulled something out of the conversation. "You said 'firstly'. What was second?"

He was looking at me strangely. "What do you remember

about Mrs Poole's?"

Shouting. My parents' angry voices. But also the crushing shame of what I had done. The stupid stories, the lies, the damage. But maybe telling him that would help.

"Not much. I remember making up all sorts of stories in my head about her doing horrible things to Evelyn. Then when Mum asked why I didn't want to go I told her what happened to Evelyn and then everything went really, really bad."

Dad was looking at me strangely. "Tell me more about Evelyn?"

Evelyn's face, blurry through time, covered in soot. Tears. "My imaginary friend. She was scared of the dark."

"Laura, there was no Evelyn." He was talking to me like you might talk someone off a ledge.

I laughed, bitterly. "Then maybe you weren't paying attention. She was the one I made up the stories about."

The zip had reached its end but there was something left in the suitcase, moving like sludge under the lid. "You were five. What five-year-old imagines being locked in a coal shed? What five-year-old would choose the name Evelyn?"

"I don't know! I don't know many five-year-olds!" My voice was getting shrill. I saw Evan put down his book and half stand. "What are you trying to tell me?"

"Evelyn was your mother's creation."

"What are you talking about?"

"Look back at the police records. I still have them. There was nothing about an imaginary friend. They couldn't find enough evidence because your mother insisted it was all a lie. They dropped the investigation and then your mother sent you back. Evelyn only turned up later, when Sandy started asking what had happened."

"No."

The little sooty face, streaked with tears. I blinked and she blinked with me. I reached up to wipe my nose and she copied me, movement for movement. Like I was looking in a mirror. Or in a reflection in the grimy window of a cellar door.

"No."

I don't know how I made it home. I think Evan shouted at my dad. There was a taxi, maybe. Callum giving me cups of tea.

I think I slept a lot.

The next day I had to go to the Community Centre to continue the preparations for the day. There was so much to do, so I couldn't afford to be slacking. There as no time for wallowing.

I arrived late and started printing off the certificates on the office computer but I couldn't keep track of how many I had done. I tried counting them, over and over, but the number wouldn't stick.

The edges of my vision were cloudy, like a darkened shroud had fallen over my eyes. Little moments, like jump-scares from some horrible movie, kept flashing into my mind. They kept catching me off guard.

I tired making a cup of coffee, tried talking to Carol about the running order, but they kept coming – during conversations, as I walked up the stairs. And each one seemed to drain a little more out of me.

A fist, at eye height.

I went to find Lillian but she was playing poker online so I just smiled and waved at her through the door.

Darkness. It was cold. I was coughing. The panic rising. Feeling my own arms, clamped around my waist. Trying to cry quietly. And then light, and a damp cloth, and promises of never again. And then darkness again.

I went into the back room and started folding programmes.

Looking into my mum's angry face. All the feelings, churning and spewing, Squash them down. Push them inside into a tiny little space, because otherwise she was always angry. Say it wasn't real. Then you get hugs. Then you get sweets.

This was no good. Maybe a day off. Maybe some sleep and all of this would simply go away. I texted Callum, asked him to come get me. I was running out of willpower.

As the message sent, a news alert flashed up on the screen. A top judge had quit at the apex of his career to volunteer in Africa. The owner of Britain's biggest media conglomerate had gone AWOL, cancelling all his meetings, and couldn't be contacted for comment.

It wasn't working. None of it was working.

Chapter Twenty-Seven

I turned over and saw three cups of tea next to my bed. When had I made those? Had I made those?

What had made me turn over? I had been staring at the wall for so long that I wasn't even sure how much time had passed.

There was a clink from somewhere in the flat. Lobster got to her feet and looked at the door. She shouldn't be pushing herself like that. She should rest. Regain her strength. If she ever could. I turned back to the comfort of the wall.

After a while someone knocked on my door. I lay completely still, feigning sleep, even when the door gently opened. I didn't want Callum seeing me like this. But it was Charlotte's voice that spoke, not Callum's.

"Laura?"

I lifted my head.

She sat gently on the edge of the bed. I shuffled around a bit to make room. Even the thought of being comforted made me want to hide away in shame.

"Hey," said Charlotte's voice. "Hope you don't mind me coming in." She put her hand gently on my arm.

I should have answered her with something cheery. Told

her I was fine. That was the done thing to do. Except that I was done with the done thing.

"If you feel up to it, I've come to get you."

For what?

"It's Hey Ewe day."

Of course it was. All that work and effort everyone had put in and I had left them all in the lurch.

I sighed. "Someone else will have to do it."

"Oh, they are," she said. "Lillian's taken care of it." That made me turn over. Her expression was more excited than it had a right to be. "And Callum is doing the MC-ing."

"What?" I sat up.

She smiled at me, only half of which looked suspiciously like pity. "He volunteered. He's been practising for days."

"He has?"

"In the kitchen. He's quite good."

"I'm sure you'll be very happy together."

She burst out laughing at that.

"Come on. Let's go see how he does."

I felt a little, tiny, mote of energy fire inside when she said that.

"I don't want people looking at me. The crazy lady."

"You're not crazy, and no one's going to look at you. We'll sneak you in the back. Lillian's arranged it all, and Callum's been briefed not to put you in the spotlight."

The mote burned a little brighter. "Promise?"

"Promise."

"Will Sandy be there?"

"No," said Charlotte. "She declined. Want to talk about it?"

I looked at her face and saw none of the frowny sneer Sandy had applied so ballistically. Charlotte was simply offering me my own mirror and would hold it up for me. I felt a wave of affection for her. All these years she had been my friend and never judged me for being too cold, too selfish, too boring.

"I thought we were friends again," I said, still a bit sniffly. "Sandy and me, I mean. She seemed to like me. And then I messed it up again."

Charlotte nodded.

"Everything is going wrong. Everything I try. It's like I'm cursed. Do you think there's something wrong with me? Am I selfish?"

"Are you?"

"Of course not!" I heard the volume that came out at and quietened myself down a bit. "At least, I'm not always."

Charlotte shuffled forward on the bed a bit. "You're one of the most self-contained people I've ever met," said Charlotte. She ignored my grimace and went on. "You never ask for help, you never share. But I don't think you're selfish. I think you expect everyone else to be the same kind of castle that you are."

I squinted at her. That was probably the most she had ever commented on my life, ever.

"So pretty self-involved then," I said.

"I think, and this is just a guess, I think you don't want to burden anyone with your problems, so you keep them locked up. Sandy does the same, but she does it out of fear."

"Fear? Sandy?"

I thought about the stitched dress. It was about being scrutinised, judged. I had been watching all these things unfold and I still hadn't understood them. All the opportunities Lobster had given me to learn, and I had taken them all for granted.

"One thing at a time," said Charlotte, holding out my towel.

It would be nice to see Hey Ewe happening. And it was only a few local people having tea. Realistically, how many people would be there. Twenty? No worse than getting on a tram.

I looked at Lobster. She had her claws up, a give-away for enthusiasm. If she could just dial the visions back, I could probably cope. Charlotte took me over to a chair. I nodded. Lobster heaved herself to her feet and launched heavily into the air.

Charlotte looked like she might dance but Lobster didn't show me anything. I had to rely on my own interpretation. Maybe she was being circumspect.

I got into the shower and gave Lobster a talking to.

"No scary circuses. Don't be showing me everyone all at once. I can't handle it. Just one at a time, OK?"

Lobster splashed and swam in the shower stream, but I think she heard me. She certainly seemed respectfully quiet in the taxi on the way over. The taxi driver had nothing unusual around him, nothing at all.

The journey seemed to take forever. Not even halfway there is was already regretting it. It was too far. I was too tired. There was no point.

We drew up to the centre, around the back as promised. I got out of the taxi and saw the door for deliveries was slightly ajar. The alley was quiet, we were alone. We'd pop in, say hi, I'd apparently magically feel great about my life again and then we'd leave in a cloud of rose petals and flying pigs.

When we opened the door into the main corridor it was noisier than I had expected. A family, at least I assumed they were from their matching coats, was walking towards the lounge. Someone, probably Carol, had hung streamers in the entrance hall. There was an easel standing near the front door but it had its back to me. It reminded me of Charlotte's, and I took her hand. She was watching me carefully and squeezed back.

I felt a bit like an invalid. I ought to be annoyed that she was treating me that way. But her hand in mine was strengthening.

The family opened the door to the lounge and a wave of noise crashed out. It was a happy noise, the noise of people having fun; of a lot of people having fun.

I found myself walking forward. As the glass doorway hove into view a whole crowd of people became visible. Were they spectres? Was this Lobster's doing?

My feet took me forward and through the door. There were hundreds of people in there. The doors to the patio were open and were even more out there. There were children running about. A man making balloon animals. A woman in a black skirt and a white button-down shirt handing out sausage rolls. She walked up to me and asked if I wanted one.

I wasn't sure how to respond. A spectre had never spoken to me before.

A hand reached past me, and Charlotte took a sausage roll. I watched her eat it.

The woman held the tray towards me, but I couldn't do anything but stare at her, even though she was apparently real. She smiled and moved on.

Carol appeared through the crowd. She was holding a box in her hands. I could see the fluffy backs of the sheep poking out.

"Hey, you," she said. She jiggled the box. "Good turn out."

"How?" I stuttered.

"Lillian," said Carol. "She's a fearful organiser when she gets going, that one."

I nodded.

Charlotte took me over to a chair.

The swirl of people went on around me. I sat with a plastic cup of tea and a biscuit and watched.

Lobster nestled on my shoulder, her weight a reassuring presence. Every now and then I would pick a person and nod towards them, and Lobster would focus on them and allow their spectre to appear.

A girl towing a balloon-unicorn on a string. As I watched the balloon transformed – a pink and white unicorn galloped behind her as she ran, its mane flowing out behind it.

A mum breastfeeding a tiny infant. Behind her a shadowy figure of an older woman had her arms wrapped around them both. And behind her another. And behind her another.

A darker shape in the corner caught my eye. Helen.

She was slumped in her same chair as always, looking down at her hands. Lost in her own gloom. As I focused the dry musty air washed over me.

I had wanted her to enjoy the day. Even a little bit. For her to feel included and not so alone.

I guess not everyone can be found. Some people are too lost in their own prisons and a party is just too simplistic a solution.

The longer I watched her the more defined her spectre was. The air became darker and drier, the colours began to leach out of the environment. A passing balloon animal flickered from pink to grey and back to pink again.

Over Helen's head a scene had formed. A dark garden. Crowded bushes and messy lawn. In the centre an empty deckchair, flapping in a blustery wind. Something in that bleakness echoed inside me like a gong. Helen's hands were moving. I squinted to see what she had but I was too far away.

Then something flickered in the garden. A shape was moving about behind the deckchair, darting this way and that. Flashes of white in the gloom. A leap brought it into the open. A lamb. It gambolled and danced, kicking its heels out behind it.

Helen was still immobile, not a twitch on her face. The musty dry air shifted, just a little bit. There was a hint of flowers. In her hands I saw a flash of white, the edge of a printed label being rubbed between her fingers.

The flowers smelled good.

"Laura." Callum's voice called me out of my staring. "You OK?"

He looked flushed but smart in his black tie. He was holding the microphone.

I wiped my eyes, ignoring his pleasantry. "I'm a bit overwhelmed by everything you've all done here."

"It's great isn't it?" He sat down next to me.

"It's amazing. Thank you."

"Thank *you*. It was your idea."

"Yeah, and then I abandoned it." I picked at the rim of the plastic cup.

"That's the thing about ideas. Once you've let them loose they're not just yours any more."

He was trying to make me feel better but it did actually sound quite profound.

"You should write that on one of the labels," I said, managing a smile.

He pressed something into my hand, then. A sheep. Its painted eyes goggled at me, slightly asquint. The label was hanging prettily from its neck. On it was written, *I see ewe.*

I laughed. A slightly choked sound.

Callum turned it over. *For a great idea*, it said in messy lawyerly handwriting.

I nodded, unable to speak.

Above him a tiny silver filigree flash of silver appeared and drifted down to settle on his shoulders.

Carol chose that moment to appear and put a hand on his shoulder, covering the thread. I felt a momentary flash of possessiveness but he had already turned to look at her.

"Sorry," she said. "Prize-giving."

"Oh, right. Thanks," he said. He got up and shrugged a smile at me.

"Break a leg," I said.

The two of them strode off towards the patio.

I turned the little sheep over and over in my hands. Such a little thing but it felt good, it felt nice. I could feel the dark space inside me thawing a little.

Charlotte appeared with a cupcake and a bag of crisps. She held one out to me and then the other. The cupcake had a little wafer sheep on it.

"Having fun?" she asked, opening the crisps.

"This is nice."

"Looks like everyone is having a nice time."

I looked over at Helen. "Yes."

"Carol said they ran out of sheep."

"Wow. Lillian had a lot of them."

"They had to print out sheep pictures as substitutes. Apparently the kids are loving colouring them in, so that's a win."

The garbled sounds of Callum over the microphone drifted in from the garden. Outside a balloon popped followed by an answering wail. Callum said something and the crowd laughed.

The lounge was starting to empty out towards the action. Soon it was only us and Helen left. A quietness descended, only emphasised by the rustle of the crisp packet. The cupcake was a little too sweet but I finished it anyway.

Helen had dropped off to sleep, her lamb curled up by her feet. The air had in it the smell of flowers, the waft of things growing and living.

A ragged cheer from outside and a round of applause.

Charlotte finished her crisps and crumpled up the bag. "So… want to stay or time to go?"

I squeezed her hand. "I'm really tired."

"Go it is, then."

"Is that bad?"

"No. It's all covered here. Come on."

As we walked towards the door I glanced out into the garden. Callum was on stage talking to a woman and a small child. He was grinning and waving his arms around. In front of the stage Lillian sat in one of the comfortable leather chairs, flanked by some of the other residents. She was laughing like a drain.

I'd thank her next Saturday. She was incredible. A power-house.

As the taxi pulled up I squeezed Charlotte's hand again. All of my friends were incredible.

In the taxi I let my head flop back onto the headrest. The journey and the stairs up to the flat were a blur. All I wanted to do was sleep. All I could focus on were the tiny pin pricks of the tiny feet of the sheep clasped in my hand.

Chapter Twenty-Eight

When I woke up the clock told me I had been asleep for sixteen hours. It was almost nine.

My limbs were heavy but everything felt soft. The pillow, the bedsheets, my brain. It was foggy and sluggish. Much better than it had been before. Noises from the kitchen suggested Callum was already up. The memory of him in his dinner jacket and bow tie made me smile.

I turned over heavily. Lobster was watching me, waiting patiently on the nightstand. Next to her was the little sheep.

I rolled out of bed and pushed my feet into my slippers. Callum had all the breakfast things out, arranged neatly on the kitchen counter, as if it were a B&B. I smiled.

"Morning," I said.

"Well, hello," he said. "Coffee? Cereal?"

"Yes, please."

He busied himself with the cafetière while I poured out a bowl of cereal.

"Yesterday was good," I said to his busy back.

"It was, wasn't it."

"How did the prize giving go?"

"Very good. Lillian won a three-wheeled motorbike tour in the tombola."

I laughed. "She'll be pleased with that."

He handed me the cup of coffee. "She was thrilled." He pushed the sugar across. "She's a big fan of yours."

"I'm a big fan of hers."

"She told me to tell you that Helen had a good time. I have to say that I couldn't see it, as far as I could tell she was asleep the whole day. But Lillian assured me that she did."

I thought of the gambolling lamb. "Lillian's right. She was better. It was better for her."

"I will have to bow to your expertise on that one. I have to say it was a lot more fun than being in court."

"You were really good."

"Thank you." He poured more coffee into his cup.

"How are you?"

"I'm fine."

He grimaced at me, in a nice way. I sighed heavily. It felt nice to get air in my lungs. "OK, I'm not fine. But I'm feeling a bit more... me."

"Can I help?"

"I don't know. But if I can think of something, I'll ask. Do you mind if we talk about something else? It's all a bit raw."

"Of course." He went to the fridge and got out a tray of eggs. "Scrambled?" I nodded.

He busied himself at the counter, breaking eggs into a bowl. "Carol had a word with me," he said with his back to me. "They're looking for a new Head of Development."

"That could be exciting." I looked at his back. "Then you could stay." The words tailed off at the end. He turned around, an expression forming around his frown. I switched to staring at my coffee cup. The inky black bubbles on the top pop one by one.

"I'm not going anywhere," he said, then. "Why would I go anywhere?"

"I just thought you said… on the canal boat. You wanted new horizons."

"In a job," he said.

A wave of relief. A misunderstanding. A smell of flowers. "Cool."

He laughed and I looked up, but he wasn't laughing at me. He seemed to be laughing at himself.

"OK, clearly the 'no pleasantries' rule is not enough. New rule. No unasked questions."

Could I do that? A million miles away from the old me. Callum had his cup raised, waiting for me to clink it.

"Not important ones," I said, and went to clink his cup.

He moved it first. "Not any ones."

I reluctantly nodded and our cups touched.

"Are you planning on getting back together with Dan?" he asked.

My snort of surprise rushed into the coffee cup, splashing it onto the counter and the tip of my nose.

"Dan? No. Why would you think that?"

"I don't know. I just thought you said… on the canal boat."

I matched his wry smile. OK, maybe I could cope with this rule. He wiped the hot coffee off my nose with a square of kitchen towel.

"Clearly canal boats are dangerous spaces," I said.

"To be handled with care," he agreed. He took a sip from his coffee. "OK then."

"OK then."

I watched him over the rim of my cup. The air seemed to shimmer silver between us.

"I have a lobster," I said. There.

His expression didn't change. He took another sip. "Explain."

I felt little butterflies start up. "She's invisible. And she flies. And she shows me what other people are feeling."

He put the coffee cup down. He looked nothing if not curious. "OK."

"You didn't know me before, but I was closed off. Then she came along. She's like a superpower. She showed me that Sandy was struggling and helped me to help her. She got me that job, and then helped me lose it again. She helped me see what kind of person Patrick was."

"Huh," he said.

It didn't seem like he was going to say anything else.

"I mean a genuine, imaginary lobster," I said. "Really real."

It would be better if he would say something else.

"That would explain a lot," he said.

The air rushed out of me. "It would?"

"Is it here right now?"

"She's just over there." I pointed. Lobster raised her feelers as is he could see her. I smiled at her. "I think she came here to show me what happened. To make me ready to hear it. I think all the saving the world stuff was a red herring."

He looked like something had occurred to him. "The politicians, the TV shows."

"Yeah."

"And are you ready now? To deal with it."

"I'm going to need help, but yeah. I think so."

He turned back to the eggs, giving them another stir then decanting them onto plates.

218

"What does she show you about me?" he asked, as he put a plate down in front of me.

"Actually, you are the only person to date that she hasn't shown me anything at all."

"OK," he looked relieved. I could leave it there. He hadn't called me crazy or run screaming from the house. That was all I needed.

"Except..." I said, before I could stop myself.

"Except?"

I felt my cheeks go hot. "Except that sometimes I think there's something between us."

He leaned forward on the counter. "What sort of something?"

"It's like silver threads. Like filigree. Sometimes they seem to connect us together somehow." I ran my fingers through the network of silver, feeling their tickle on my hand.

"Sounds beautiful." He was smiling.

I leaned forward onto the counter too. "It is." I reached out and took his hand and the glittering strands flowed down onto our hands and resolved themselves into a single silver thread.

"OK then," he said, grinning like a fool.

"OK then," I said, ignoring Lobster who was dancing in the corner.

Chapter Twenty-Nine

Something about that conversation gave me the courage to video-call Mum the next day. She seemed pleased to hear from me and immediately launched into a story about her neighbour next door.

Behind her the doilies appeared to have bred – tiny white puffs crowding on every surface. The little wizened gnome on her shoulder was also firmly in its place. It was settled into a raggedy bundle, with only its little pointy ears and the tips of its eyebrows showing.

She changed tack, unexpectedly. "Have you spoken to Sandy?"

"No. She's still not talking to me. Why? What's wrong?"

"Probably a good thing for you. She's gone crazy."

"What happened?"

"I don't know. The same thing that happened with you, probably. She's behaving like a crazy person. I honestly don't know what to do about her anymore."

"I'll talk to her."

"If she'll take your call. Maybe she'll cut us all off. Just like your dad."

I looked away from the screen, reminding myself that this sofa was a friendly sofa, that this flat was a safe space, this phone call could be ended by simply pressing a button. I was already tempted.

I looked over at Lobster. She was watching me quietly. Her calm seemed to radiate throughout the room, helping me.

It was now or never.

"Mum, I need to talk to you about something."

The gnome's head appeared out from its bundle.

"Well, that sounds serious," said Mum.

I eyed the gnome. It didn't look worried.

"I want to talk to you about Evelyn and Mrs Poole."

She stopped then, entirely still. For a long moment, I thought the screen had frozen but then I saw her blink.

The other thing I saw was the gnome slowly pull itself to its feet on her shoulder. Its expression was thunderous. The same light shone in my mother's eyes. It stepped to the side, so instead of being cuddled into her neck it was raised to its full tiny height. As it did so, out from behind my mum's back came its other hand. It was huge, comically big, like a deformed catcher's mitt. Was it going to try and punch me through the screen?

Lobster launched herself off the table and came and settled on my shoulder. We were ready to go, head to head.

I breathed out and let the words flow out of me. "You told me that I made it up, that it all happened to my imaginary friend. But it didn't. Mrs Poole was cruel and... she hit me, Mum." The words somehow came out intact.

My mother took a breath and her eyes widened but as she formed her mouth to speak the gnome's giant hand came racing around from behind her and slapped across her mouth.

Instead, the gnome formed words and my mother's mouth followed. "Not this again."

I felt myself sag down in my chair. Only Lobster's reassuring weight on my shoulders let me continue.

"I wasn't lying."

The gnome snarled and the glove tightened its grip. Behind it, my mother's skin was going white. Her eyes were wide.

"Why are you dragging up the past," said the gnome in my mother's voice. "Haven't we all been through enough?"

I felt the familiar tightening in my chest. The pressure to sit back, bow down, be quiet. I pinched my nails into the palms of my hands and kept going. "I know you want to keep the peace. I know you did the best you could at the time. I don't blame you. But I need you to understand what happened to me. I didn't make it up. You told me it never happened but it did."

Now her eyes narrowed. "You made up little stories to get attention." She was breathing heavily. "You destroyed our family with your dramas and nearly destroyed a lovely woman's reputation in the process. I forgave you because you were too young to understand what you were doing. But you're a grown-up now."

The words felt like echoes. Once in the flowery bedroom at the top of the stairs, once in the kitchen with Dad railing and shouting, once in the hallway of the therapist's office, once in the mediation room that smelled of peppermints, once in the new house where I shared a room with Sandy and everyone told me to just stop.

I felt myself shrinking back as she continued, years of terror and shame threatening to drown me. But this time Lobster showed me something new. Behind my mother was a faint

222

copy of her, hovering half in and out of sight. She was half-sized and picked out in shades of grey like a faded cinefilm. She was beating her hands against an invisible wall. Tears were rolling down her cheeks and she was and shouting words I couldn't hear.

Every time my mother said something that broke my heart a little more the shadowy image beat the walls a little harder.

The gnome saw me staring past them and looked from the shadow mother back to me. Its grip tightened.

"Stop!" I yelled.

Mum fell silent. Her tiny shadow-self rested her head against the invisible glass, staring at me, tears pouring down her face. I wanted to reach out to her. I wanted to feel her arms around me, hear her voice in my ear. She was right there, not three feet away, begging to get to me.

"Please can you listen to me. I don't blame you. I just need you to tell me you believe me. That you know that what I'm saying is true. I need my mum. Please, please be my mum."

But between me and her was the gnome and a lifetime of denial.

Her voice was cold. "Mrs Poole was a saint. You have no idea what that woman's husband put her through. She had nobody in this world."

"I understand," I said, my knuckles gripping tightly to the table.

"You do not understand. How could you understand being betrayed and left alone? You have no concept of how hard it was for women in those days. She had three children and no other income. Everyone turned against her. Everyone. I was the only person she had. What was I supposed to do?"

"You were supposed to protect me."

223

"You were fine," she scoffed. "A little bit of discomfort never hurt anybody."

The ghost of my mother put her head in her hands and sobbed. I found myself putting a hand against the cool glass of the screen as if I could reach through it and get to her.

"I think somewhere deep inside you know that what I'm saying is true," I said slowly. "I think you know it."

She had to believe me.

The gnome shifted its grip. A nasty smile came into its eyes. "I know you believe it's true," my mum said. "You were just a child, a fanciful, stubborn child, and you told so many stories that you can't tell the truth from your fantasy anymore."

As she spoke the image behind her started to fade. Lobster shuffled forward on my shoulder. I felt her feet grip hard and heard her claws grind together with effort. The gnome released its grip and its gloved hand fell away but my mum continued on all by herself. "Children's lies can feel so real, imaginary friends, dreams that feel like memories, nightmares that haunt you for years. I understand you think it was true." The image behind her was fading almost to dust. I cried out but my mum carried on. "But that's quite enough nonsense and I'm done listening to you."

The faded version of her was gone. Lobster collapsed on my shoulder. It was no use.

I took a breath. "I hear what you're saying. I'm sorry that's what you think. Until you are willing to listen to me, I won't be spending any more time listening to you."

"What are you saying?"

"I need to take a break from you. I won't be calling for a while, and I won't be coming to see you."

"Oh for god's sake, this is ridiculous. I can't have both my children refusing to talk to me, what will my friends say?"

"I'm sorry, Mum, but this is what I have to do."

"You are ungrateful. I'm done talking to you. Goodbye." She hung up the call.

I slumped back on my seat, Lobster scuttling over my chest and hands anxiously. I was shaking. I should be crying, howling, heartbroken. But it felt like something inevitable had just happened.

I felt weirdly light, weirdly free, like I could leap up from the sofa and join Lobster in her flying around the room.

Callum wouldn't be home for half an hour. I had the place to myself. I poured a large glass of wine and simply allowed myself to breathe.

Chapter Thirty

I texted Sandy and asked her to meet. I said I was sorry about before and that I needed to make it up to her. While I was waiting for a reply my phone rang.

I answered it, thinking maybe it was her. It wasn't. It was Barry.

"Hi, Laura. How are you?"

"I'm fine thanks, Barry," I said, keeping it light. "How are you?"

"I, er, I heard what happened with Tom. Sorry."

"Thanks. But it's fine. I don't think that place was for me."

"Well, I didn't want you to be left in the lurch, so I was calling to say, if you want your job back, it's yours."

What? "Won't that get you into trouble with Tom?"

"Maybe. But it wouldn't be a bad thing for something to happen around here that he doesn't like. And he doesn't have control over who I hire and fire."

I thought about the call centre, my jeans and hoodies. The life I had left behind.

"Just 'til you find something else if you like. You're a solid worker, and the figures you were totting up before you left are much missed."

Was I still that person?

Yes. Yes, I was. I still liked jeans and hoodies. I missed the scripts and the busyness. I liked going to the cafe for lunch every other day. I had plenty of new things in my life to wear me out. Some old things would be nice to have too.

"That would actually be great, Barry, thank you."

"Great, see you Monday?"

"Thanks, Barry."

"My pleasure," he said and hung up.

My phone buzzed. It was from Sandy. *See you tomorrow at 2. Usual place, S x*

The bistro was mostly empty when I sat down at our table. Sandy was late. For our entire lives, she was always the one that was early. I thought about what would cause all this lateness. It had started before our argument, so it wasn't just that. Something had been wrong for a while and I had been too blind to see it.

As I looked over the menu I felt my nose tickle, then was overwhelmed by the most god-awful smell. Like something had died. It was pungent, earthy, septic. Where was it coming from?

I looked up and saw Sandy had come in. At least she didn't have to smell it, but I was going to look stupid if I was pinching my nose. I tried not to breathe too hard. Maybe the person whose spectre this was would leave soon and let the fresh air back in.

As she came closer the smell got stronger.

"Hi," she said, brightly. "Did you order yet?"

She took off her coat and hung it on the chair. The smell came and settled around us like a blanket made of dog faeces.

"What's wrong?" I asked.

She looked up from the menu. I saw a whole range of emotions cross her face. I could name them, one by one, but now I knew what was driving them. Above all she was afraid, and she was most afraid of looking like a fool. But she was my sister and she couldn't resist it when *I* looked like one.

"Something is rotten in the state of Denmark," I said, darkly. I raised an eyebrow and gave her a dramatic baleful glare.

She spluttered a laugh then; it had a hint of tears about it. She fought it back and glared at me, mock disapproval at my silliness. Her smile lasted a few seconds and then she buried her head in the menu again.

The waiter appeared. As usual, he turned to her in her smart suit with her lovely hair. I ordered for both of us to save her having to speak.

When he'd gone I said, "I'm sorry about last time. I wasn't paying attention. I'm here to listen now."

She nodded, still studying the menu. "Mum has stopped talking to me."

"I know. Why is it this time?"

"It's Alan."

Oh god, what had he done? If it was cheating, I was going to kill him and bury him in the river. I waited.

"He's got a problem," she said, through gritted teeth. "Gambling."

Not what I was expecting.

"It's been going on for years. Before we met, even."

Alan. Respectable, Rotarian Alan. Alan who I hadn't seen much lately. "When did you realise?"

"Two years ago. I went into our savings account and it was gone."

Two years! The thought of Sandy, the bright superstar, struggling under the weight of this for all that time was too bizarre.

"Have you been dealing with this all on your own since then?"

"No, I told Mum. She found him a counsellor. I thought it was fixed. I thought it was fine. Then two months ago I found a pile of credit cards he's been hiding from me."

"Oh, Sandy."

"Well, what did I expect when I married a Sagittarius?" she said. We both laughed to give her some relief.

Our drinks arrived, then. She placed her hands around her cup and stared at her herbal tea. The stench was easing a little and I was able to take a sip of mine.

It was now the time, the script, to ask 'why didn't you tell me?' But it felt like the wrong time and it's not like I didn't know. Years of hiding from each other, pretending we were close, pretending we were normal sisters. If she had tried to tell me I would have run a mile. Just like when I had tried to tell her and she had done the same.

"I'm sorry I didn't say anything," she said. "Before. I felt embarrassed. Stupid. And, you just have to put on a brave face, you know."

As she said that the stitches on her top glowed brightly. I glared at them, "You don't have to," I said.

She shrugged at that and sipped her tea. What could I do? Should I hug her? Give her an arm punch? There was a range of possible reactions. Instead, I looked at her with lobster-eyes. The threads were still glowing brightly and the stench was still strong.

I reached across and took her hand. "With me," I said. "You don't have to pretend with me."

She looked up then. She smiled at me and squeezed my hand and let go. The smell finally died back to a gentle pong; a skunk on the horizon.

"What are you going to do?" I asked.

"He's agreed to go back to counselling again. He's embarrassed too. But it's the debt that's the problem. It's going to take years to dig ourselves out of that hole. Mum flew into a rage when I told her. She said he was bringing the whole family into disrepute. She says she won't talk to me ever again unless I leave him."

"I'm so sorry, Sandy."

"It's not your fault."

"I know, but I'm sorry it's happened anyway. Can I help?"

"No, no, don't worry about it. You don't need to do that. It's his hole, he needs to fix it." She smiled ruefully.

"You still love him."

"I do. He's struggling, but he's trying."

The food arrived then and we made the right noises at how nice it looked and then ate in silence for a while. How tired she must be. How sad. It wasn't fair.

"Thank you for telling me," I said.

"Thank you for not judging me," she replied.

"Of course I'm not going to judge you. I'd still like to help."

She waved my words away. "How did it go with Dad?" she asked.

My heart thumped painfully in my chest. But if she could, so could I.

"It was difficult."

She made a noise in her throat. "I hope you didn't let him confuse you," she said. "He's a narcissistic liar."

I felt myself bristle but was distracted by a shape forming

on her shoulder. A shrivelled, hunkering shape which glared at me with baleful eyes.

The gnome. Or a smaller, slightly transparent, version of it shuffled forward a little, establishing its rightful place. Passed down from mother to daughter.

How many generations did this thing go back?

Maybe this was a bad idea. Maybe this fragile connection was all a sham, and this would just be Mum all over again.

No, this was Sandy. She was caught up in this, just like I was. I could make her understand.

"I think he wasn't lying," I said to the gnome.

She snorted and took a breath to retort but I put my hand over hers first. She looked up in surprise.

"Do you remember Evelyn?" I said.

She narrowed her eyes for a moment then realisation dawned. "Your imaginary friend?"

"Yes, her. What do you remember about that?"

"She was like a coping mechanism or something." She was looking at me, back and forth from eye to eye.

"That's what the psychologist said," I nodded.

"She was a disaster, wasn't she? Always getting hurt. Always the victim." I felt a cold shiver trickle down my spine but kept her gaze. "She told you to lie about Mrs Poole."

"I think I was Evelyn."

"Of course you were Evelyn, she was your imaginary friend."

"No, I mean she was me. I invented her."

She was staring at me, hard. "Of course you invented her; she was your imaginary friend, she repeated."

As I watched, the gnome started getting to its feet. It was tugging hard on its other hand, trying to raise it. I watched as it pulled and pulled, a sneer and then a scowl on its ugly face.

It wasn't long before the giant hand appeared. Translucent as it was it still looked brutish and real. Not again, I prayed.

"I invented her to replace me, inside my head. To replace me in what was happening to me."

"Happening to *you?*" She was searching my face. Maybe looking for the joke. "But Evelyn was locked in a cupboard all day."

"A coal hole," I said, quietly.

Her hand flew to her mouth. Her head was shaking, *no.*

I gave her a rueful smile.

The gnome took a step forward and swung but as it did she jolted forward and took my hand. The gnome slipped and stumbled and then fell. It disappeared behind her shoulder and I heard a diminishing shriek.

"I'm so sorry," Sandy said.

Then I was laughing. Gulping, tearful laughing.

She believed me.

"It's not your fault," I said, between gulps.

She squeezed my hand. "Except that this one sort of is."

She was completely serious. That sobered me up.

She said, "I should have protected you.

I took her other hand and squeezed. "No, that wasn't your job." *It was Mum's.* But I didn't say that.

"I should have tried."

"No, listen. Think about it. Dad tried and he got kicked out of the family. You had no choice but to believe it was all in my head or you might have been kicked out too."

She shook her head. "No, Mum wouldn't have... Dad didn't..."

Then something else occurred to her. "Oh, I'm making this all about me. How are you? Are you OK? God, you've been living with this for years. No wonder you were—" She caught herself, horrified.

"No. It's OK. It's true. No wonder."

"I don't mean it like that. I just mean…"

"I know. But I've found a therapist. I'm getting help."

"I wasn't kind to you."

I shrugged. What to say to that?

"I'm so sorry."

"Thank you."

We were sitting across from each other, both hands clasped. She was smiling at me, sadly. I felt like a weight had gone from my shoulders.

I had been worried she wouldn't believe me. It was nice to have her look at me and really see me. At least, that was what I assumed she was feeling because it was what I felt, what Lobster allowed me to feel.

"What a mess we both are," I said.

She laughed then. So did I.

Things would be different. I had someone who understood, who had been there. I could see her brain working, revisiting all our memories, just like I had.

What would she do about Mum? What about Dad? Would she be willing to meet him now?

Everything would be different. Everything I had ever feared. People could see me. I wasn't invisible anymore. But instead of feeling terrified, I felt something lighter. A balloon, or a kite. Something colourful and dancing. Hope maybe.

Chapter Thirty-One

I let myself into the flat. Callum was watching TV but he switched it off and came over when he saw me. He kissed me ever so lightly on my lips. The silver threads thrummed like harp strings.

"How did it go?" he asked.

"She believed me," I said. I felt like dancing.

"That's great," he said and kissed me again. "How do you feel?"

"I feel like a huge weight has been lifted. I feel like I am seeing things more clearly. I feel like maybe I can forgive myself."

There was the sound of a splash.

"Because it wasn't your fault?"

"Because it wasn't my fault." The words tasted strange in my mouth.

Then I saw it. From the edge of my vision, there was the crest of a wave. A white tip breaking against the coving in the corner of the room. What was happening?

The waves sank a little lower and I realised there was a water level at the top of the room. It was sinking fast. I felt my stomach drop.

"Oh no."

"What's wrong?"

"I'm the fish," I said to him. "I couldn't see the water, because I'm the fish." Who was I telling, me or him? No wonder I hadn't seen it before. Of course I couldn't get Lobster to show me my spectre. How do you show water to a goldfish in a bowl?

Lobster hovered near my face, her legs stroking rhythmically. She wasn't flying, she was swimming. She tucked her tail under and did a little flip. I felt the wash from it caress my face.

The wave near the ceiling bucked a little against the pillar and as I watched the water level drop.

"No," I said. I sank into my chair.

But lobster merely did another cartwheel. She was happy.

"No."

It seemed to be the only word I had left.

"You OK?" asked Callum. He tried to lift me to standing but I pushed his hands away. The water was draining, the surface was getting nearer and nearer.

Would it hurt? Would I suffocate in the harsh air? The water had reached the tops of the door frames. Just looking at it seemed to make it go faster. I shut my eyes, wanting to sink to the floor and crawl under the table. I had to stay down, in the water, with her.

Lobster came over and settled on my hand. Her feelers stroked the edges of my palms in that familiar caress.

Please, no.

It had reached Callum's head. He emerged, unknowing, into what seemed to be painful whiteness. All clean and shiny and bright.

"She's leaving," I cried at him. I sank lower in my chair and pulled Lobster close. The surface tickled the top of my head.

I threw myself onto the carpet but Lobster scuttled beyond my grasp, into the middle of the floor. A noise next to me and then Callum was sitting there with me, holding my other hand.

There wasn't a place low enough to escape it. I pressed my cheek to the floor and reached out my hand, but Lobster merely reached up on her tiptoes and took a little bow.

The surface dipped below my eyes. Gasping for air like a fish out of water. The haze of the water dropped away, and the light and sound came crashing in like a filter had been dropped from all of my senses. Lobster looked at me, from under the last inch of water, through the ripples from my breath.

The level sank beneath the floor and she was gone.

Epilogue

I have an offer for you. This envelope contains one of lobster's eggs.

It's not for everyone. It's a process. It's something I didn't even know that I needed. But I'm glad I knew her and grateful to her every day for what she did for me.

Things aren't easy still. It's only been a month since Lobster left and I feel her loss like an agony. But, unlike the metaphor, I don't feel like I've lost part of myself, I've gained back a whole side of me that I had lost. I don't always like her. She's emotional and makes bad decisions. She's really angry. We're getting to know each other, rubbing along.

Callum is helping.

I haven't spoken to Mum. I don't know what to say. I guess she did what she thought was right but also, fuck her.

What I'm offering is painful. Some people run away from it. Others embrace it. It's up to you really. But if you do it, I can promise you it will change you forever. It's not the world, but it's a start.

Over to you.

Love,

Laura x

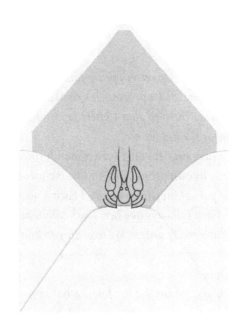

About the Author

Erica likes to tell people she learns for a living and writes for fun. With the help of the many talented writers around her she, for some reason, very much enjoys closeting herself in a room with imaginary people and letting them surprise her with what they say and do.

A single mum to the best thing she has ever done and a grateful resident of Scotland for over 25 years.

You can connect with me on:
- ⊕ http://www.dean-park.com/ericamanwaring
- 🐦 http://www.twitter.com/ejsj
- 🅕 http://www.facebook.com/ericamanwaring

Also by Erica Manwaring

Notes From a Physicist Lost in Time and Space

Dr Alison Howden has devoted her life to understanding the base rules of the universe, the ones that hold even in multiple universes. If she can just understand how everything works then she maybe will find it easier to live by her one rule: never go back on a promise. Especially her marriage vows.

Then Jack explodes into her carefully controlled life. He reveals that all her theories are true - he's from another universe. But his world is crumbling. He can save them but he's trapped in Alison's universe and only she can help. She agrees to go with him, determined to save them and tempted by the promise of seeing the multiverse for herself.

Jack promises he'll bring her back home. Or perhaps to a more perfect version of home - one where keeping her promises isn't quite so hard. All she has to do is hold her nerve, trust him and take the leap.

Printed in Great Britain
by Amazon